Based on a True Experience

A Ring Doesn't Make the Marriage

A Ring Doesn't Make the Marriage

Consuelo Danita

Publisher: Consuelo Danita

A Ring Doesn't Make the Marriage is a work of fiction and while names of businesses, locations, and organizations mentioned may exist, the story is solely fictional. Likewise, characters are fictional and in no way speak for any person.

Paperback ISBN: 978-0-9994926-1-1

Library of Congress Control Number: 202190173

Printed in the United States of America

Cover Photos by Alexander Diaz
Atlanta, Georgia

Dedication

To Felipe

Thank you for believing I could create a simple story with weighty principles that would benefit any relationship.

Chapter 1

Can a good marriage come in different colors? He said, "I love you." She said, "I love you too." And then sometime later they both said to each other, "I do." Then, why is it not working? The main reason is because of several underlying factors, problems, problems, and more problems. The second reason is that they did not have a clue on how to solve the problems.

The small-town wedding was simply charming. The bride walked down the aisle, dressed in an ivory colored, long sleeve lace ballgown with a v-neckline. One other item that captured the attention of her ensemble was the satin ivory stiletto sandals that wrapped around her chiseled ankles. The fitted bodice of the ballgown accentuated her hourglass shape or as they say in the South, her 'Coca Cola bottle figure' that clearly spoke to her femininity.

In particular, she carried one long stem ivory colored Calla Lily tied with a three-inch yellow satin ribbon with pearl accents. Along with her outfit, she styled a beautiful pinup at the base of her neck with a couple of long tendrils around her face plus a few at her nape area. She clipped to her ear a pair of teardrop earrings made with a pearl surrounded by crystals. Her makeup transformed her into an artistic portrait, even though, she did not need anything added to her flawless face. Absolutely stunning, she moved cautiously like walking on rice paper down the red carpet in a backyard filled with floral arrangements of red as well as yellow roses.

The bride's maid of honor wore a sleeveless pinkish lavender chiffon dress with a low-cut back, which draped slightly over her well-defined back muscles and sculpted arms. The beaded belt fit snugly around her tiny waistline above her caved-in abdomen, giving the appearance that she may have done five hundred sit ups each day for the past year. Besides her windswept curly hair pulled to her right side, everything about her depicted youthful innocence.

She had picture-perfect dark eyebrows, enhanced by glowing dark skin. The only makeup she wore was a soft pink lip gloss. Her svelte figure caused the dress to talk. "Look at me." Because she preferred low heels, she wore brilliant iridescent ballet flats with crystals that saturated the toe cap. Also, there were crystals dotting the sides including the heel for extra sparkle. She locked her fingers around a bouquet of yellow roses, red roses, baby's breath, besides a sprinkle of greenery.

The groom plus the best man wore an ivory-colored suit with a soft lavender bowtie made of silk. Each pinned a boutonniere to the lapel, made with olive colored greenery infused with baby's breath around the yellow rose. The groom's shaved head brought attention to his focused eyes and pearly white teeth that he flashed when his bride walked toward him.

It was a perfect day. Fluffy clouds painted the beautiful blue sky with a temperature of seventy-two degrees Fahrenheit. There was peace all around. Their families yearned for this young couple to marry a few years ago, but they remained silent. And now the families' hope was on the brink of fulfillment.

Long before this wedding occurred, the bride, like many Southern girls looked forward to getting their first hope chest. This chest brought about a turning of age in a young girl's life, with the goal of preparing for marriage.

Two young teenage girls who lived in the same neighborhood was about to get their hope chest. Marylou Marshall and Jasmine Summers who were neighbors, about five doors down from each other in a subdivision in Monroeville, Alabama, a small Southern town near Mobile. Marylou was about five feet, eight inches tall with an olive skin tone, complemented by her brownish red hair. Her eyelashes and brows were thick. She had smiling eyes. On top of that, she had a small beauty mark on her right cheek and a larger one on her left cheek.

Jasmine was about five feet, eleven inches tall, dark skin tone with dark brown hair. Her smile was delightful. She had a small space between her two front teeth that she hated because it was an old saying in the South that 'if you have a space between your two front teeth, you were a liar.' Although it was the cutest gap, she despised it. Both girls had a soft Alabama twang when they spoke. They were so close until at times, they completed each other's sentences.

They were in the ninth grade, and both had turned fifteen years old in May, within three days of each other. They would become sophomores in the fall. The girls were excited about finally getting a hope chest, the chest that they would use to store their valuable things in for their future marriage.

Marylou's momma, Missy Marshall, was thirty-nine years old. She got married at twenty-one years old, right after she graduated from college. She had a side of her that was fun and energetic, although, she revealed that side sparingly. Being very particular about the hope chest that she would get for her only daughter, she had a local carpenter make the chest of cedar with decorative copper designs placed on the top of all four corners of the chest. The primary request Marylou wanted more than anything else was a lock with only one key, where no one else had access. And that is what her momma got for her.

Jasmine's momma, Cashmere Summers, was a thirty-six-year-old, divorced, single working mom with two teenagers. Her skin color was pecan tan. She had an athletic build which made you think that she could have played sports. Jasmine was not as fussy as Marylou was because she knew that her momma could not afford a lot. Cashmere was able to give her daughter an antique suitcase with a worn-down exterior that she had painted a very pretty lavender color, along with a yellow rose in the center of the hope chest.

Her momma combined dried lavender with lavender essential oil and placed them into sachets that she placed inside Jasmine's hope chest to lessen the old smell of the redecorated suitcase. Like Marylou, the lock was also important to Jasmine. Though there was not a workable lock on the suitcase, Jasmine's momma gave her a pink spray-painted chain with a lock and key that Sam, her older brother, had used to tie his bicycle to the tree in the backyard before someone stole it.

Since the mommas of the two girls were also close friends, each of the mommas placed the same gift in each daughter's hope chest. Each daughter had a small notebook with the title written: "My Wedding Planner." This is where Marylou and Jasmine would write down specifics about their ideal future wedding.

They would write notes to answer questions like: Where do I want to get married? How many people will I invite? What type of wedding will I have? What will I wear? What kind of ring do I want? What is my dream honeymoon? What kind of husband do I want to marry? Where do I want to live? Additionally, they would put girly pieces of lingerie, and other dainty items, as well as other memorable keepsakes into the hope chest.

The other item that each of the mommas left in the hope chest was a copy of the Bible. You see, the South was known for being the 'Bible Belt' of the United States of America. Each momma had positioned an embroidered handkerchief with the teen's first name to serve as a bookmark for Matthew chapter nineteen. Highlighted in pink, verses five, six and seven poetically read: "For this reason, a man will leave his father and his mother and will stick to his wife, and the two will be one flesh. So that they are no longer two, but one flesh. Therefore, what God has yoked together let no man put apart."

Marylou and Jasmine were ecstatic that they were about to satisfy the Southern tradition of stuffing their hope chest with precious gifts, as they made the journey to their ideal marriage.

In the girls first conversation, they discussed what they would wear to their wedding. Marylou wanted an elegant ivory colored dress with a fitted bodice, along with a flowing bottom from the Bridal Shop in Mobile, Alabama because there was no Bridal Shop in Monroeville where they lived. Jasmine wanted a knee length country wedding dress along with mid-calf cowboy boots. Besides loving that style, she reasoned that she could order it online from Amazon. For that reason, they decided to collect photos of various wedding dresses to put into their individual hope chests.

Their mommas, Missy and Cashmere, were about to jump out of their skin as the girls invited them to help find photos to put in the chest. It was such a beautiful time for the mommas and their daughters to experience this project together during the summer vacation. After a couple of months, though of looking through different catalogs, the thrill ended. They all had to get back to their old routine of getting ready for the new school year. Summer was now over.

Chapter 2

The school year was tough for Marylou and equally tough for Jasmine. They were sophomores in high school. Both had aggressive although different schedules. Plus, they began to spend less time together at school. In Marylou's quest to become a journalist, she set out taking advanced classes to prepare her for college. Jasmine had gotten really good at playing basketball with her older brother, Sam, who was seventeen years old. He also provided the lock to go along with the chain for her hope chest. Jasmine felt that shc was a pretty good basketball player; therefore, she tried out for the varsity basketball team. She made the team. Of course, she was not surprised. She was confident that she could make the team.

Marylou ended up taking one of her journalism classes at the local community college where she met a young man from the neighboring county. His name was River Parish. He was also a sophomore in high school and the assistant editor of his high school newspaper.

River looked like he was a mix between Hawaiian and Black. He had lightly tanned skin coupled with light brown eyes. He was about six feet, two inches tall. Among his stellar appearance and thick curly hair, he had a soothing voice which allowed him to effortlessly imitate certain vocalists. He loved to sing, dance, and pretend on occasion to be a tall Bruno Mars. He flashed an infectious smile. Marylou and River had one more thing in common. They both knew the Summers' family. River and Sam were friends.

About two weeks into the course, the teacher assigned a project to the class. Marylou, River, together with two other classmates worked on the project. Marylou had not talked to Jasmine in several weeks. When she stopped by her house to let her know what was happening in her class at the community college, Jasmine was shocked.

Not only was River a friend of Sam, but Marylou also learned that River was their cousin. That was way too much for Marylou. Jasmine could not understand why Marylou was not excited. She was not pleased that River left out that detail. Troubled by that fact, she would not let it go. In other words, she beat it to death.

Jasmine asked, "Marylou, did he not tell you that he was related to us, that we were cousins?"

"No, he said that he was your brother's friend."

"Well, that's true. Maybe their friendship held more weight or was more important to River than saying we are cousins. I am sure he did not think anything about that. So, do not make a big deal about it. I do know that they are good friends and have been since they were very little. Have you ever left out a few details to get to the bottom of a conversation, which to you means not telling the complete truth?"

"I guess so. Perhaps I was over reacting Jasmine."

"You say, 'Perhaps I was overreacting.' You are my best friend. I know you are leaving something out. What is it?'"

"Like what?" Marylou asked.

"Like you are interested in him."

"Jasmine, I have only known River for a couple of weeks. Yes, I am interested; however, I don't want to go out on a date with my best friend's cousin."

"A date?"

"I mean Jasmine…you know…we are working on this project together. We are getting along great. That could happen."

Jasmine grinned. "Sure, it can. Are you going to write his name as a candidate for being your husband in your Wedding Planner book?"

Marylou answered, "Much too soon to tell. What

if I do? Whose business is it?"

"Not mine Marylou because I have my own business."

"Oh yeah. What do you want to tell me? What is your business? Is it related to basketball?"

Jasmine took a deep breath and slowly exhaled. "There is an intern who is working with Coach Van Damme. He is his nephew. He told me that I have a lot of potential."

Marylou's eyes got big. Then she blurted out, "Which means that he must be in college or have completed college. Right?"

Jasmine looked around to see if anyone was listening and said, "That's right. He's in college."

"What is wrong with you Jasmine?"

"Nothing is wrong with me Marylou. He watched us practice. He helped me with a few drills. I am not sure if he likes me. He is so kind and patient with me. He keeps telling me that I'm really good and keep it up."

"His name is Tommy Van Damme."

"Tommy?"

"What does he look like?"

"Marylou, I don't know. Average. He is about six feet, two inches tall or three inches tall, athletic looking. He has sort of dreamy, sleepy eyes. Really laid back I would say."

Marylou scolded Jasmine. "You and Tommy could get into deep trouble!"

Jasmine responded in kind. "Why do you think that could happen?"

"Because you are fifteen years old. He must be over eighteen years old if he is in college. If he has graduated from college, he is probably twenty-one years old. That is against the law!"

"Whose law Marylou?"

"The government!"

"Marylou, you don't know what you are talking about."

"I don't? Then tell me what I don't know."

"For starters. He finished high school at sixteen years old because he was home schooled. He started taking college classes online. His uncle is spending time with him because he loves basketball. That is what I think."

"Well Jasmine, you got me all worked up because you didn't tell me the whole story. You are just like your cousin."

"Ok Marylou. You are a sore loser. Ha!"

"Ha back Jasmine! Are you going to write Tommy in your wedding planner?" Marylou roared.

"Not at all! I am going to bed. I am getting up in the morning, going to school and after school, I am going to basketball practice. I will tell you what else I find out about Tommy and his goals before I write him in my book. How do you like that?"

"Well go ahead then. Go drill him."

The girls ended the inquisition. Marylou hugged Jasmine and went home. Her momma met her at the door when she arrived. She said, "Marylou someone named River has called for you three or four times. He said it was urgent and to call him as soon as you get in. Where were you?"

"Momma, I stopped by to see Jasmine. I am sorry I did not tell you. I had to tell her what was going on in school. She had to tell me what was going on with school too."

"Who is River?" Marylou's momma asked."

"I'm working on a class project with him in addition to two other classmates. He is related to Jasmine and her brother."

"Ok. Well, hurry. Call him back. Then we can have dinner."

Marylou dialed River's number. He picked up on the first ring. "Where have you been? I have been trying to reach you all evening. Are you okay?"

She broke in. "I went by to see my best friend Jasmine, who is your cousin by the way."

"I thought you might have done that. I am sorry I did not tell you I was related to the family. Jasmine's brother knew that we were in the same class. He thought it was better to tell you we were friends instead of cousins. I really did not agree with him; but I went along with it, because well you know, he knew you longer than I have. I apologize I did not tell you the entire truth. Will you forgive me?"

"River, I must admit I was quite disturbed when I learned that; however, Jasmine reasoned with me. She convinced me that I should not make a big deal out of it. So, I forgive you."

"Thank you. Now I can rest easier. I never want to withhold the truth from you again. I will see you tomorrow. Have a good evening."

Marylou hung up the phone. As she walked to the kitchen to wash her hands for dinner, her momma inquired, "What was so urgent to River?"

"Momma he wanted to tell me he was sorry because he did not tell me that he, Sam and Jasmine were cousins. Sam thought it would be better to tell me that he and River were friends. Can you believe

Sam told him I was always overreacting about different things? He never knew what would send me off."

"Well Marylou that is a very honorable thing for River to do. He must really respect your friendship. I can see why Sam told him that. I remember the time when you got mad with him because he said something about the outfit you had on. Oh, and that your hair looked a little off."

"I know that time I went off. It was a bad day. I also think that River respects our friendship momma."

"Let's eat. It is just you and me today. Your daddy and brother will not be here for dinner. We can talk about your day if you like."

"I would like that very much momma. What did you make for dinner?"

"I baked a small turkey, sautéed green beans, baked sweet potatoes and tossed a green salad. You can have ice-tea or lemonade. If you want to, you can take some of the turkey for your lunch tomorrow. Would you like that?"

"Yes, I would. That sounds yummy for my tummy mummy." They laughed.

"Marylou, would you like to say the prayer tonight?"

She said the prayer. They talked for hours about what happened in one day. Missy enjoyed every morsel of building an intimate relationship with her daughter.

Chapter 3

Marylou got up early the next morning. Refreshed after a good night's sleep, a great dinner, and a chat with River, she was ready to finish working on her class project while eating a light breakfast. River was waiting for her when she arrived at the college campus so that they could walk to their class together.

All at once, River said to Marylou, "I like you a lot. Although I have only known you for two weeks, I would like to take you on a date for ice cream."

"River, I like you too. I would not mind having ice cream with you; but my momma and daddy said that I cannot go out on a date until I am sixteen years old. Besides that, my parents or my brother has to be a chaperon."

River smiled, "That is okay with me Marylou. When will you turn sixteen?"

"In May."

"Will you promise me that when you turn sixteen years old, you will choose me to be the first one you go out with to get ice-cream?"

Marylou asked, "Will I be the first one you go out with on a date?"

River said, "Yes, I have never asked anyone else to go out on a date."

Marylou could not wait to get home. She fled to Jasmine's house to tell her what had happened. Jasmine could not believe that River moved so quickly to ask Marylou out on a date. More than that, she was surprised that he was willing to wait until she turned sixteen years old, which was seven or eight months away, an eternity for Jasmine. Lastly, Marylou told her momma about her day. Although her parents had promised that she could begin dating at sixteen years old, her momma was surprised that it was happening so quickly.

Missy kindly commended her daughter for explaining to River their wishes. Following the discussion with her momma, Marylou scribbled in her Wedding Planner. River Parish could be a possible marriage mate.

In the meantime, Jasmine got a chance to talk with Tommy about his goals and desires. Tommy wanted to coach high school basketball. He wanted to get married, have children and settle down in Monroeville. For whatever reason, his response did not settle too good with Jasmine at the time. She never expected to live in Monroeville after high school. She wanted to get married only because that was the norm for Southern girls, especially in Alabama. The reality of talking about marriage frightened her. She wanted to play professional basketball. Maybe later get married.

Jasmine, like Marylou, rushed home to talk with her

momma about Tommy's interests and goals. Her momma seemed pleased. She did not understand why Jasmine did not feel the same way. Maybe she had taken that professional basketball goal a little bit too far, being a small-town Southern girl. Instead of writing Tommy in her Wedding Planner as a possibility, she wrote, "I don't feel the same way about marriage after talking about it to Tommy."

Winter break had arrived. Everyone was talking about their winter plans. Marylou and Jasmine had gotten permission from their parents to visit Marylou's grandparents in Florida. Near her grandparents' house was a three-day basketball camp. Marylou went with Jasmine to the camp each day from nine in the morning until noon. After the basketball camp ended each day, they went to Coquina Beach to swim. The three weeks in Florida were truly refreshing for the girls.

Two days before Marylou and Jasmine were about to leave Florida, one of the lifeguards at the beach literally bumped into Jasmine. He apologized as he held her to keep her from falling down. He looked into her eyes and said, "I think I've seen you before. Were you at the three-day basketball camp near Tamiami Boulevard?"

Jasmine answered, "Yes, I was."

He added, "My name is Skyler Chadsworth. I saw you when I stopped by the basketball camp. I came in to watch for a while. I saw you hit a three-point bucket from the side with your left hand. And it was beautiful. You are too."

That was a lot for Jasmine to handle. She looked over at Marylou, then looked at Skyler and said, "Well, thank you. We have to go." The girls rushed away. Skyler threw multiple questions at Jasmine while they were walking away.

"Hey! Why are you leaving? What's wrong? Where are you going? Are you coming back? At least tell me what your name is?"

"My name is Jasmine Summers. I'm going back to

Alabama Friday afternoon."

"Alabama? What part?"

She disclosed, "Near Mobile."

"My daddy is from Alabama. He played football at the University of Alabama at Tuscaloosa. I will be playing basketball there in the fall."

"In the fall? How old are you Skyler?"

"I'm seventeen. I will be eighteen in July. How old are you?"

"I'm fifteen. Well, Skyler, it was nice meeting you. Maybe I will see you in Alabama. Have a good day."

As Marylou and Jasmine ran away giggling, Skyler yelled, "See you in Sweet Home Alabama!"

The girls did not expect to see Skyler again. But they did. He had checked afternoon flights leaving the Sarasota-Bradenton Airport on Friday afternoon going to Mobile. He found one. He decided to go two hours early to the airport to wait for them. As he roamed the entrance to the airport, he saw the girls. He ran toward them. As he got closer, he yelled,

"Sweet Home Alabama Girls." They turned around and saw Skyler running toward them. They waited on him. When he got closer, he said, "I wanted to make sure I got your telephone number Jasmine. Mobile is a big place."

Jasmine replied, "My number? Why should I give you my number?"

"That's not a good question. Can we exchange numbers or email addresses? I promise I will not harass you."

"Like you just did?"

"That's a good one Jasmine. I know that was a little over the top to come to the airport. That was my last chance to find you. Listen, you can block me if I get on your nerves."

"Ok. I will give you my momma's number. I don't have a cell phone."

"That's great Jasmine! Here is my number and my email address. I will call your momma tomorrow. Please be sure to tell her that I will be calling."

The girls looked at each other as Skyler said, "Don't want you to miss your flight. Talk to you later Jasmine. Have a safe trip back to Mobile." After the girls marched through the airport to check-in, Marylou broke her silence.

"What was that all about? That was creepy, don't you think?"

Jasmine looked Marylou dead in her eyes and answered, "He had a whole lot of spunk. But I tell you one thing Marylou, if he calls my momma tomorrow, I may consider writing his name in my wedding planner."

Marylou replied, "For real?"

"Yes, my dear friend Marylou. For real."

"What if he doesn't call you tomorrow Jasmine? Will you be upset?"

"Not hardly. He's gonna call."

Concerned by what just occurred, Marylou probed more. "How do you think your momma is going to react to his call?"

"I think she will be surprised because I'm not going to tell her he is going to call. I'm not telling her anything concerning Skyler."

Marylou hollered, "You are not going to tell her?"

"Nope."

"Uh-wee Jasmine. You are begging for trouble."

"Well Marylou, the way I look at it, it's both of them that will be surprised. I wanna get a chance to see how both will handle it. If it is good, I will probably write him in my planner."

"Girl, you are crazy! Crazy! You hear me!"

"Marylou, you better keep this to yourself. Do not say a word to your momma or daddy. You hear me."

"Yeah Jasmine, I hear you. Always remember that I warned you. What about Tommy? Have you forgotten him?" Marylou asked.

"Who? What about Tommy? I am not writing him in my planner. No, not right now anyway unless he changes his goals. Not interested in living in Monroeville. You worry too much. May the best person win."

Marylou sighed, "Hmm. Ok. Ms. Thang. Let's rest on the plane. You have a long day tomorrow. I would be having a hissy fit if I were you."

Jasmine said, "Honey why don't you write a song with those rhymes you just had."

The girls slept like they had taken a sedative. The flight was about ninety minutes long. It seemed like they had only slept ten minutes, when it was the entire flight.

Chapter 4

Missy and Cashmere rode to the airport together to pick up the girls. The mommas asked questions. "How was your plane ride? Are you hungry? Are you tired?"

Jasmine's mom commented, "Seems like you have lost weight Jasmine. Was the camp a lot of work?"

Jasmine whispered, "Momma, of course it was a lot of work. It was also a lot of fun."

"What was the best part of the trip?"

Jasmine uttered, "Momma, the best part was the basketball camp for me. I know for Marylou it was going to the beach because she watched me at camp."

"What happened at the beach Marylou?" asked Jasmine's mom. Jasmine was smiling at Marylou.

"What happened? Well, we had a great time. The sand was beautiful. The water was perfect. We went swimming. We left."

"Did you girls meet other young people?" Jasmine's mom continued.

"Of course, we did. I cain't remember them all." Marylou replied.

Marylou's mom concluded, "I guess that is enough conversation for today. You two seem very exhausted. You can get some rest and give more exciting details tomorrow."

Both girls were no doubt thinking that within twenty-four hours, Skyler would be calling Jasmine's momma. Both girls insisted on going to visit some of their school friends so that Marylou would not feel the pressure of possibly letting the secret out.

In the meantime, Skyler was really looking forward to talking with Jasmine's momma. Although, he was strikingly handsome, it never went to his head. He really was a down home country guy. He was the type of guy that often visited his elderly neighbors. He loved chatting with them to find out what life was like when they were younger. Amazingly, he hit it off with them. They always looked forward to spending time conversing with him.

Although Jasmine thought that it would be challenging perhaps for Skyler to talk to her momma, that was far from being a challenge for Skyler. The only challenge you might say he had with the call was that he did not get the name of Jasmine's momma. Actually, he was looking forward to speaking with her momma because he was an excellent conversationalist.

Skyler dialed the number Jasmine gave him about four p.m. The phone rang three maybe four times. Jasmine's momma answered, "Hello."

Skyler spoke up, "Mam, my name is Skyler Chadsworth. May I please speak with Jasmine's momma, Ms. Summers?"

She said, "I'm Jasmine's momma. Why are you

calling?"

"Jasmine said I should call you. I apologize that I did not get your full name from her. That is why I asked for Jasmine's momma, Ms. Summers. I wasn't sure if there were other females living in the house."

"Well, that's very nice of you son. My name is Cashmere Summers. Why did Jasmine ask you to give me a call? Is she okay?"

"Ms. Summers I'm not sure if she is okay. She told me to call you because she did not have a cell phone."

"When did she tell you that?"

"Yesterday, when I talked to her at the Sarasota-Bradenton airport."

"I tell you Skyler. That daughter of mine is a hoot. She has a cell phone. She was probably playing a joke on you and me. How did you meet her?"

"I met her at the beach. In fact, Ms. Summers, I almost knocked her down when I bumped into her. When I looked into her eyes, I asked her if she had attended a basketball camp near Tamiami Boulevard.

She said yes. I told her I dropped my friend's sister off at that camp. I saw her hit a three-point jumper from the side. It was beautiful. I told her she was beautiful. We talked a little while longer. Then she said she had to go."

"So, what took place when she told you to call me?"

"It wasn't right away. We had talked about when she was going back to Alabama. I remembered that she said she was coming back to Alabama on Friday afternoon. I looked up all the flights going to Mobile Friday afternoon. Later, I went to the airport looking for her."

"Son, how old are you?"

"I'm seventeen. I will be eighteen in July. That is what Jasmine asked me also. I asked her for her cell number or her email address. I told her I would not harass her. She said she did not have a cell number. I should call you. Did she tell you that I was going to call you?"

"No, she didn't. As I told you my daughter is a hoot. She probably wanted to see how you would handle it."

"Do you like my daughter?"

"Yes mam Ms. Summers. I do like her. I told her my daddy was from Alabama. I was going to play basketball at the University of Alabama in Tuscaloosa in the fall."

"Skyler, what do you want me to do?"

"Please give me her cell phone number. Please do not tell her I called. I will call her later tonight. Would that be okay with you Ms. Summers?"

"Skyler, son that would be absolutely all right for me and fun for you to do that. You are spot on. She'll get a piece of her own medicine."

"One last thing Ms. Summers, Jasmine is beautiful. I'm sure she got it from her momma."

"Skyler, I hope so. I am older now. But when I was younger, we looked alike. What part of Alabama is your daddy from?"

"He's from Mobile."

"Mobile? What is his name?'

"Luke Chadsworth."

"Luke Chadsworth? Did he play football for the University of Alabama?"

"Yes, Ms. Summers he did. Do you know my daddy?"

"Sort of. When he was in high school, his football team came to play against my high school. I was a cheerleader. I talked to him after the game. I think he was a senior. Small world, isn't it? How is your dad?"

"He's doing ok. He and my mom got a divorce. So, he has been working a lot.

"Where is he working?"

"At the University of Alabama."

"I'm sorry that your parents got divorced. My husband and I got a divorce when Jasmine was thirteen years old. That has been hard on Jasmine. How are you doing with the divorce?"

"I'm doing ok. I live with my mom, so when I go to college this fall, I will live with my daddy or in the college dorm. I have not made up my mind yet."

"I'm sure that your parents will help you to make the right decision."

"Oh, I think so too. Ms. Summers, I think about things that young people do not think about. When I get married, I do not want to end up like my parents. I think about things like that even though I am not old enough to get married. My mom tries to help me keep a healthy view of marriage. She says not all marriages are the same. What do you think?"

"I think your momma is right Skyler. It is what you make of it. A marriage must be a union of two people that love each other, united by similar values and goals. Foremost is that each person should be a good forgiver. I have learned that the hard way. By the time I learned it, it was too late. Well Skyler, it has been nice talking to you. I'm sure you don't want to stay on the phone with an old lady."

"Ms. Summers, I enjoy talking with people older than me. I visit my neighbors in Sarasota-Bradenton, Florida all the time. That is how I learn. That is why I ask for their opinions because I value what they have to say. A lot of them say they like talking to me."

"That's wonderful Skyler. Well, I hope you can carry out your little joke on Jasmine. Nice talking to you. Have a good evening Skyler."

"You too, Ms. Summers."

Cashmere really considered Skyler as a potential marriage mate, although it was ultimately up to Jasmine. She was set on playing professional basketball; although Skyler seemed like he had a well thought out plan, Jasmine would evaluate his goals and desires. Jasmine showed Cashmere that she had gumption and she was excited that Skyler was no push over. He knew what he wanted, and it was her daughter.

Chapter 5

It was around five thirty in the evening when Jasmine came home. Upon her arrival, her momma commented, "Jasmine you must be exhausted catching up with all of your friends. Did you see everyone you wanted to see?"

"Yes momma. Marylou and I even went to see some of her friends. She did not have as much to talk about because she did not participate at all in the camp. Not much went on at the beach."

"Ok. Yes, it would have been different if it were during spring break instead of winter break. But, glad you are back at home. What would you like for dinner?"

"A grilled cheese sandwich would be great

momma! How was your day?"

"Well, your brother was gone all day like you. Anyway, I caught up on all of my household chores when I made it home from work. Decided to take a little nap. A little peace and quiet is wonderful when you can take it."

"So how was work?"

"It was busy. I worked on six large floral arrangements for several banquet tables and a few smaller arrangements."

"Did any of your friends call you momma to see how you were doing while we were gone?"

"No. You know I don't get a lot of people calling me. I would prefer to go visit people and they come to visit me before I call them on the telephone. You know how I am. I just remembered that I did get a call from someone. It was strange."

"Who was it, momma?"

"Not sure baby. They hung up when I said hello, hello. Then I called back to see who it was.

Somehow, I disconnected after two rings because of how I was holding the phone. Very strange still. It was as if someone wanted to talk but got scared. I didn't dial the number again because I was really trying to finish what I was doing. Well, that was the excitement for me. Other than that, it was quiet."

"Did the person call back?" Jasmine asked.

"No. Honey were you expecting someone to call?"

"Me? No, not really. I sort of hated that I left you here all day long after I returned from Florida without telling you how my trip was."

That's okay Jasmine. The person who called probably figured that it was the wrong number when they heard my voice. What do you think?"

"Maybe so momma."

"You sound sad Jasmine. Baby what is going on?"

"Nothing momma. I'm a little tired."

"Yes, that's probably it. You have been in Sarasota-Bradenton for three weeks, basketball camp three of those days, went to Coquina Beach every day and then the very next day after you arrived home, you stayed out all day visiting your friends. Clearly, you are too tired to talk to me about your visit to Sarasota-Bradenton. Do you want to eat now?"

"Maybe later momma. I am going to take a quick shower. I'll eat after that."

"We can catch up at dinner. Grilled cheese it is!"

Jasmine took her shower, put on her bed clothes, and sat down to eat her grilled cheese sandwich. She had almost finished it when her phone rang. She said to her momma, "Not sure who that is. Marylou and I are all caught up talking."

Jasmine's momma said, "It's still early. Maybe she forgot to tell you something."

Jasmine answered the phone without looking at her caller id. "Hello Marylou. What did you forget to tell me? Tell me quick because I am ready to go to bed."

"Hey Jasmine. This is Skyler Chadsworth. How are you doing?"

Looking back at her momma with her eyebrows

raised and her eyes stretched wide open, Jasmine asked, "How did you get my number?"

"Skyler answered, "Your momma gave it to me. Didn't she tell you I called?"

"No, she didn't. She said she had one call. It was a hang-up. I guess that wasn't true."

Skyler cleared his throat. "Why did you tell me you did not have a cell phone?"

"I didn't feel comfortable giving my number to you."

"Do you think what you did was honorable for a person who wants to play professional basketball?"

"I suppose not. I had just met you. I am only fifteen years old. I don't have a lot of experience giving my number to strangers."

"Not to be rude Jasmine, so why did you give me your momma's number if you did not have experience. You seemed like you have a lot of experience testing people."

"You are absolutely right. I wanted to see if you

were afraid. I see that you were not afraid because you convinced my momma to give you, my number."

"Jasmine, I really enjoyed talking to your momma. She was very kind; nevertheless, she was surprised you forgot to tell her that I was going to call. How did you forget that?"

"Since we are being honest, I just wanted to see how you would handle the phone call to my momma. Also, I wanted to see how she would handle it. I didn't forget to tell her."

"You know, Ms. Summers said you were a hoot!"

"My momma told you that?"

"Ask her."

"Hold on a minute." Jasmine muted her phone. "Momma did you tell Skyler that I was a hoot?"

"No Jasmine. I told him you were a bit snooty when you wore your little country booties, then sometimes shouting because you were moody if someone hit you on the tushie, as you were leaving basketball practice with your favorite hoodie."

"Momma! You have jokes. No, you did not say that. Did you?"

Cashmere smiled. "Would you believe the truth if you heard it?"

"How could you do that?"

"Do what?"

"Make that little rhyme about me."

"Jasmine have you ever been moody?

"Yes. Everyone has been moody one time or another momma. But you told him that and he doesn't know me really well."

"Jasmine, I am not finished. Do you wear country booties?"

"Yes, you know I do momma."

"Do you wear a hoodie when you leave basketball practice?"

"Yes. Yes. Yes."

"And finally, my dear daughter. When you were in the sixth grade, what did you do to the little boy that slapped you on your tushie? I am waiting. I'm tired of waiting."

"I twisted his arm behind his back."

"Was there anything about that rhyme that you didn't understand?

"You made your point. I guess that I can forget about talking to Skyler anymore. I am going to tell him I gotta go."

"Why honey?"

"I am too embarrassed that my momma made that type of rhyme on me."

"Yes, honey bun, I'm joking. I told him you were a hoot. That is it. You probably wanted to play a joke on both of us. Isn't that what you were doing? See how it feels."

"Yes, momma. It didn't feel good."

"Go ahead and talk to Skyler for a little while. We have to go to our spiritual service at eight a.m. tomorrow."

"Ok. Thank you, momma."

"I'm back Skyler. I am sorry it took so long. My momma was asking me a few questions that I needed to answer. What else did you talk to my momma about? Please tell me everything."

"I told her she must be beautiful because you are."

"You told her that? How long did you talk to her?"

"We talked about ten minutes."

"Now, that you have my number, what are you going to do with my number Skyler?"

"I'm going to lock it in my phone and put you on speed dial. Would that be okay?"

"Well, I guess so. Seriously, don't call me every day."

"No, I want. The days that I do not call you, you call me."

"For what?"

"So, we can talk."

"Not at all Skyler. I am busy with school and basketball. I cain't even talk to my best friend every day. Maybe once in a while I can talk to you. If you cannot do that Skyler, I will block you. I'm serious."

"Yeah Jasmine. I understand. It's no problem. Let's check-in once a month. I can call your momma to talk to her the other days. She told me that I was smart and mannerable."

"You wouldn't dare call my momma every day."

"I would because your momma said she enjoyed talking to me. I enjoyed talking to her too. I like talking to older people. It helps me to learn. I can call you every Saturday to talk for about five to ten minutes unless we have more to catch up on."

"You are so persistent. Well, I talk a lot about basketball."

"Perfect subject for me too Jasmine. Talk to you next Saturday. Have a good evening. Please tell your momma thank you again for the nice conversation and your cell number."

After Skyler and Jasmine finished talking, Jasmine started questioning her momma about the conversation with Skyler.

"Momma, how long did you talk to Skyler?"

"Sweetheart, it was only probably about ten minutes. Beyond a doubt, he has very good manners, very open and honest."

"I cain't believe you gave him my number. I cain't believe you momma. Uh! Uh!"

"I cain't believe you gave him my number young lady without telling me. Listen, you like basketball. Skyler likes basketball. Tommy likes basketball. Seems like a pretty good combination of friends talking about the game of basketball that you love. You can have Sam join in also. All of you can get together to talk about it online. I am going to bed. Please clean up the kitchen. Then go to bed. We will leave about seven twenty in the morning. Oh, by the way, do not forget your prayer tonight. Include a request for forgiveness of what you did to me and Skyler. Then think seriously about the blessings you received today and thank God for at least three things before you say amen. Is that clear?"

"Got it Momma. Have a good night."

Jasmine finished cleaning the kitchen. Right before she got ready to say her prayer, she decided to text Marylou.

"Marylou, momma and Skyler played a trick on me. She figured out that I was playing a game when I did not tell her Skyler was going to call. So, she gave Skyler my number. He called me."

"No way Jasmine!"

"Way."

"Not only that Marylou, she likes him, and Skyler said that my momma wanted to talk to him another time. I think I might write him in my planner. I can always erase him."

"Jasmine, what about Tommy?"

"I think I might write him in my planner too. I can always erase his name. It's not like I'm getting married anytime soon."

"That's right Jasmine."

"Gotta go. Good night."

Jasmine knew her momma did not play when she told her to pray before she went to bed. So, she got on her knees and in prayer to God kindly asked, "Please forgive me for playing with my momma and Skyler. Thank you for my life. Thank you for my parents. Thank you that I got a chance to go to a basketball camp. Thank you that I have a hope chest."

Early the next morning, Jasmine got up to fix breakfast for her momma and brother. What a surprise for them. She opened a can of biscuits, put them in the oven, scrambled eight eggs and cooked six pieces of bacon. She had jelly on the table, orange juice along with a small pitcher of water. No one in the house drank coffee. Jasmine's momma and brother approached the kitchen sleepy eyed and hungry because of the smell of the food.

Sam asked Jasmine, "Why did you make breakfast today?"

"Don't I do this every now and again?"

Her brother responded, "It's like never ever."

"Come on yawl. Jasmine made us a nice breakfast. Let's sit down, eat it and enjoy it."

Jasmine responded, "Thank you momma. I hope you like it."

The breakfast was delicious. Jasmine's brother cleaned the kitchen while the girls finished getting ready for their spiritual service. After their spiritual service, they got home in time to take their good Sunday clothes off and put on casual clothes when the phone rang. It was Cashmere who received the call.

"Hey Ms. Summers. How are you doing? This is Skyler Chadsworth."

"Hey. I'm doing well. What is on your mind today?

"My momma is an only child. I am too. I was wondering if you would be okay if my momma gave some items to Jasmine."

"What kind of items?"

"My momma said every Southern girl has a hope

chest. She still has her chest. She wanted to know if you would like to give it to Jasmine with some of the things that she never used."

"That's very nice of your momma. Jasmine has one. But I am sure she could use it along with the one she has. Let me ask her."

"Jasmine this is Skyler. His momma has a hope chest with several items in it that she has never used. She has no daughters or other girls in her family. Skyler's momma wants to give it to you. Do you want it?"

"Momma, I like what you gave me."

"Now honey, it will not hurt my feelings."

"Let me think about it momma. I will tell you tomorrow. Tell Skyler to please tell Mrs. Chadsworth thank you. I need to think about it."

"Yes darling. I will let him know."

"Jasmine's mom whispered, "Skyler, my little baby girl wants to think about it. I do not think she wants to hurt my feelings. She said she will let me know tomorrow. Do not give it to anyone yet. Jasmine wants you to please tell your momma thank you. Will you do that please?"

"Okay Ms. Summers. I will tell momma. Please call me as soon as Jasmine makes up her mind. Momma knows how special Jasmine is to me. She will not give it to anyone else."

"Will do Skyler. What is your momma's first name?"

"It's Liz. Because I told my momma how beautiful and sweet Jasmine was, she thought she would really like it. She doesn't mean to offend you or Jasmine."

"Oh, I'm not offended. Your momma has not met my daughter. If I know my little girl, which I do, your momma's generosity stunned by your."

"Well, have a good evening Ms. Summers. Talk to you later."

"Thank you. You too Skyler."

After Jasmine's momma hung up the phone, Jasmine asked a question. "Momma what do you really think?"

"Jasmine, you have been a good girl. That is God's way of letting you know he cares about you. Skyler is impressed with you and no doubt he communicated that to his momma. And if he is a momma's boy, she really wants to make him happy."

"Momma, thank you. I will make my decision tomorrow. Once I have done that, I will call Skyler. You do not have to call him. I will accept this responsibility. Got to grow up and not be afraid of what she will think of me."

"That is very commendable."

Jasmine tossed and turned all night long. She struggled with making a sound decision that would make everyone feel better. Several times under her breath, she murmured, "How can I make everyone happy? How do I do that God?" Jasmine questioned what if she accepted the gift, what would her momma truly feel about her decision; especially after her momma had worked so hard to construct her hope chest. This gift was essentially one of a kind. On the other hand, if Jasmine rejected the hope chest, Skyler's mom may have felt that Jasmine had no idea of how precious that chest was to her and that she was willing to give it to someone that she had never met. Another possibility was that hope chest may have contributed to negative feelings between Jasmine and her momma, along with her momma feeling that she was not able to supply something precious for her daughter, but someone else did. Since Skyler made the call, he may have been embarrassed. Jasmine hoped for a good night's sleep with a solid decision in mind by morning.

Chapter 6

The very next morning, it was clear in Jasmine's mind what she wanted to do. She did not discuss it with her momma before she called Skyler. He answered, "Hey Jasmine. How are you doing?"

Jasmine replied, "I'm well. I wanted to tell you that I have decided what to do. I would like to have the hope chest and the things that are in it."

"That's fantastic Jasmine! My momma will be so delighted. That is one of her most special treasures."

"Skyler what do I have to do to get it?"

"Nothing. My momma can ship it out today."

"That will be great. Please send it to the Post Office in Monroeville. Ask them to hold it for pick up. If you do not mind, please put my phone number on the box, so that the Post Office can notify me when it comes. I'll call you when it arrives. Skyler, thank you. Please say thank you to your momma. Please do not tell my momma yet that I accepted the gift. I want to tell her at the right time."

"No problem Jasmine."

Cashmere had assured her daughter that it would be okay with her if Jasmine wanted the chest. She was counting on her momma not changing her mind. She finished getting ready for school, ran into the kitchen to grab a Danish and a piece of fruit when her momma walked into the room.

"Jasmine did you make a decision?"

"I have momma, but I'm going to wait before I tell you. I called Skyler to tell him I had decided."

"So, what is your decision?"

"I have to think about a couple more things before I have it firm in my mind."

"You are talking in circles. In other words, you

still have to decide."

"I have decided momma. I need to know how to carry it out."

"You are more confused than I thought. Is Skyler and his mom aware of your decision?

"To a degree."

"Don't mess with my nerves. His momma was very kind."

"Skyler understands I want to be sure."

"Young lady, I'm giving you a week to settle this in your mind."

"Okay momma. That is more than enough time. Trust me please."

Skyler's mom mailed the hope chest on Monday. He called Jasmine to let her know that it would arrive on Wednesday. Just as Skyler had said, the mail carrier called Jasmine for pick-up on Wednesday. She asked Marylou to pick it up and keep it hidden. Then, she would meet Marylou later at her house. When Marylou picked up the box, she told her brother it was for a school project. She placed it in her closet until Jasmine would come to open it. The girls locked the door, quickly opening the package. When they saw the hope chest, it was like a princess had owned it. It was extremely attractive. It appeared to be about the size of an average toolbox.

Several items were inside the box. There was a package of white lace handkerchiefs, a pair of white gloves, a journal with a pen set. Moreover, in the box was a small cushiony manila envelope that read on the outside in caps: **DO NOT OPEN UNTIL YOU HAVE SET A DATE**. So, the girls had gotten this beautiful wrapping paper from the dollar store. They left everything in the box except the envelope. Jasmine called Sam to come over with some of his art paper and colorful pen set. When he arrived, Marylou directed him right into her bedroom.

Jasmine asked him to write three sentences on the art paper in calligraphy with beautifully colored artwork around it. It looked amazing as he completed it. Jasmine put it into the envelope. Then she carefully placed the envelope in the chest.

The girls struggled to tie a big silver bow on the gift-wrapped chest. They stored it in Marylou's closet with a big blanket on top of it to hide it with some of her clothes that she had not hung up in her closet. They both pulled out their study books. They sat at the table in the dining room so that they would not bring any attention to what they had been doing in the bedroom.

When Marylou's brother walked by, he asked, "Are you going to work on your project that you picked up today?"

"Marylou said, "I have to take it to school on Monday."

"Oh ok. So, you are early. That is good. See you soon. I am going out for a while. Please tell momma I'll be back in time for dinner."

"I will tell her; but you better be back, or she is going to have a temper tantrum."

"Don't worry about it. Would you please tell her what I told you?"

Sam waited about ten minutes after Marylou's brother left before he exited quickly through the back door. The girls studied together for about an hour. Then Jasmine went home. She asked her momma if she were still upset with her.

"Jasmine, I'm not upset. I'm concerned that you may not be sensitive to other people's feelings."

"Momma, I'm sensitive. I called to tell Skyler. He would have called you if he wanted more information. He was content with what I said. I am happy that you are not upset with me any longer. I promise that I will be responsible. You will see."

"Know that you must decide by Monday. Today is Wednesday."

"It will be momma."

"Momma is a little tired. Would you mind getting dinner for us tonight?"

"What would you like momma?"

"How about a fried baloney sandwich with mustard?"

"Momma I can make that in about fifteen minutes?"

"Well, you probably ought to make one for your brother too. He can heat it up if he isn't here when you finish."

"Okay momma."

When Jasmine finished frying the baloney, her brother walked into the kitchen.

"Smells good in here. So, Jasmine are you the chef tonight?"

"Yes, and you are the dishwasher."

"Don't be so mean."

"Mean? When was the last time you prepared food for momma or me?"

"The last time you had the best meal ever."

"Looks like Jasmine has everything prepared, let's all sit down to eat. Good. Jasmine you prepared a little side salad. Everything looks good."

"Thanks momma."

"So, momma, Marylou and I have been working on a project. It is at her house. Can we show it to you Friday evening?"

"Sure, what kind of project?"

"It's a secret."

Jasmine's brother asked, "Can I see it too?"

Jasmine looked at him, blinked her eyes several times. "Why do you want to see it?"

"Because it might be fun."

"If you want to come, you must come when momma comes. Deal?"

"Yeah, deal. The sandwich is very good. Thank you. I will wash the dishes."

"Outstanding! Thank you, big brother."

Jasmine's momma asked, "Will Marylou's family be there?"

"I'm not sure momma. I think maybe her momma will be there."

"Oh, it's no problem. Curious somewhat."

As they finished the meal, Jasmine asked, "Momma why are you so tired tonight? Did you have a busy day?"

Before she could answer, Sam agreed, "Momma I noticed too that you were unusually tired, tonight. Is everything ok with you, your job or is it something else?" To their surprise, she mentioned something that she had never said before.

"I had the worse day I have had in a long time. When I left work, I saw your daddy. I said hello. He walked by me with his new girlfriend. He did not say one word."

Sam said, "Momma, I'm so sorry that happened to you. That wasn't nice."

"It's been a little over two years since he left. I thought we both had moved on with our lives. I see now that he moved on and I had not done so. Just to ignore me, the momma of his children, it was too hard to bear. They looked refreshed, no stress, no worries. By contrast, I was tired, no makeup, hair ungroomed.

Why did he have to see me like that?"

Jasmine tried to comfort her momma. "Momma remember Skyler said that you must be beautiful even though he had not met you. I know you are beautiful because a lot of people say I look like you. They say I am beautiful too. Momma you have natural beauty. You are a hard worker. Daddy saw you at the end of your day. Don't be sad please."

"Yeah baby. I know you are trying to cheer me up. But when I got into my car to come home, I turned on the radio. One of Whitney Houston's songs came on: *Where Do Broken Hearts Go?* Your daddy and I always argued about little things. I thought about the big blowout argument that we had the night he walked away from me, from us.

"Shortly after that song played, another song came on by Al Greene: *Let's Stay Together.* Yeah right. I had hoped your daddy would come back; but he did not. By that time, Al Greene had finished singing the song. When I wiped my tears with my left hand, I scratched my eye. It was a little bit of a scratch because I had my wedding ring on that your daddy gave me. I did not notice that I had not taken it off. In two years, I had not taken it off. I thought to myself, "Why do I still have this ring on? Why? For what? It did not help our marriage. He has someone else. Then I removed the ring from my finger. I broke down.

"In addition to that, during my twenty-minute ride home, I started thinking about when I met his parents. How they helped me prepare for the wedding. How they talked to me about marriage. How effective communication was vital to a marriage. Not to go to bed angry. They helped your daddy pick out my beautiful engagement ring. Maybe that is why I did not take it off. It was the second most precious thing that I had next to you two.

"Your daddy thought I was beautiful once. After two children plus endless arguments, he wanted something better, someone else better than me, I think. I guess. I am disappointed that I really have not moved on. The ring was all that I had left of a chance to reunite. I think trying to hold my emotions back, really exhausted me."

"Momma you are only thirty-six years old. You got married at eighteen years old. Had Sam at nineteen years old. Had me at twenty-one years old. You can have a better life too. I firmly believe that in my heart." Jasmine declared.

Sam reinforced what Jasmine said, "I also agree with Jasmine Momma."

"Kids, I really feel bad that I have burdened you with my feelings, my problems. I'm so sorry."

"Momma, we love you. We are a family. Good things are gonna happen for you. I am excited about our surprise for you on Friday. Maybe that will cheer you up."

"Yes. Maybe so. I have something to look forward to. I'm excited about it."

Encouragement was what Cashmere needed. She

was determined to change her life and she was on her way to accomplishing her goal.

Chapter 7

Cashmere got up early Friday morning to prepare for work and her surprise that Jasmine planned at Marylou's house after she left work. She started by taking her hair down from the one braid that she normally wore to work. After she shampooed her hair, she put a few rollers in her shoulder length hair to polish it off. Just the smell of the shampoo was uniquely invigorating for her because she knew something special would happen later in the evening.

While sitting under the hooded hair dryer, she painted her nails a pretty pastel color, which was a little different from her regular routine. After her hair dried, she put a little mascara on her eyelashes which gave the appearance that her eyes were wide open. Next, she boosted her morale by putting on a peach-colored lipstick that she hardly ever wore. She sprayed a little mineral water on her face to give her perfect skin a dewy look. Then she called out to the children to come and see her miniature transformation. When they heard the call, they pushed the half-opened door to her bedroom to peek in. There standing in front of the mirror was Cashmere Summers.

Sam said, "Momma, you look like you are twenty-five years old. What did you do? I have not seen you look like that in a long time. Even when you go to the spiritual service, you do not look like this. What happened?"

"I did what I needed to do for some time. I got up to take care of myself. You two know how to cook, clean, not to mention other tasks like washing the dishes, ironing, cutting the grass, taking out the garbage, and taking care of yourselves. It is time for momma to make some changes. Jasmine was right. I am still relatively young. I do not have to carry myself like I had been doing. I am happy that you like what I was trying to do."

Jasmine, intrigued by her momma's dewy pecan tan skin said, "Momma you are gorgeous. I'm so proud of you."

"Sam and Jasmine, I needed to stop defining myself by a ring on my finger. Now, it is off. I am going to have a new attitude. I am excited about my surprise tonight. This is a start to show my appreciation, my desire to make changes. I must leave the past. When I thought so much about the past, I could not focus on the present time. Neither could I think about my future, our future."

Sam was so off the chart. He got his phone. Took a selfie of the three of them. He said, "Momma, that's what I'm talking about! Look at you. Change is good. I want you to be happy. It would make Jasmine very happy too."

"Jasmine and Sam, I'll be home around five p.m. Sam, please wait until I get home. We can walk down to the Marshalls' together. I'm going to wear a very pretty dress that I have not worn in a long time."

Jasmine said, "Momma, I'm so excited because I cannot remember the last time that I have done something for you. I hope you like what I did."

"I'm sure that I will sweetheart. Have a fabulous day at school. I will see you both later."

Sam encouraged Jasmine. "I know momma will really like your surprise. It is going to do so much for her self-esteem."

"I think so too Sam, especially after I saw what she did with giving a little attention to herself."

Jasmine and Sam left for school together. When they got to school, she saw Tommy. She was going to say hello; but she noticed that Tommy's face looked strange. He did not see her. As she got closer to them, she heard the girl he was talking to say, "What are you going to do? I have not told my parents. When I do, they need to know what your intentions are?"

"Tommy said, "My intentions? I do not have any intentions. I am sixteen. I really do not know you. My parents would be upset with me. I cannot afford to hurt them."

"What about me?"

Jasmine had not seen this young girl at school. What was she talking to Tommy about? Jasmine decided to go up to them.

She got right in his face. "Hey Tommy. What is going on? You were not at practice for the past two days."

The other girl sarcastically asked Tommy, "Who is she?"

Tommy replied, "This is Jasmine. She is on the women's basketball team."

Jasmine asked, "Are you new to the school?"

The young lady looked Jasmine up and down. "I don't go to school. I graduated last year from high school. I live down the street around the corner from Tommy. If you do not mind, I really need to finish my conversation with Tommy."

Jasmine replied, "Sure, no problem. I will see you later Tommy."

As Jasmine walked away, she looked back at the two. She noticed that Tommy hugged the young lady and said, "We can work this out. Just give me time to talk to my parents."

Jasmine waited until after the young lady walked away. Then she approached Tommy. She demanded an answer. "Why were you acting strange Tommy?"

"I wasn't acting strange. She is a troublemaker. I was trying to convince her to give me time to talk to my parents."

"She seemed pretty upset Tommy."

"Yes, I was too Jasmine."

"Well, I hope it gets better after you talk with your parents. By the way, I have a surprise for my momma this evening; therefore, I will not be running the optional drills we have today. Would you please remind coach that I told him that yesterday?" she asked.

"I sure will Jasmine. Have fun with your momma tonight. Have a good weekend."

"You too!"

Jasmine at once called Marylou on her cell. When she answered, she asked Jasmine if everything were ok. Jasmine went on to tell her that something strange was going on with Tommy. He looked awfully scared. She also said that there was another girl talking to him that had graduated from high school. That was strange also.

Marylou said, "That's not strange. You said Tommy graduated from high school at sixteen. So maybe she did the same."

Jasmine responded, "She looked a lot older than sixteen years old."

"What do you think is going on Jasmine?"

"I think that girl is pregnant. She came to tell

Tommy. I heard part of the conversation. He told her that he was sixteen. He also said he had to talk to his parents. That spells trouble to me. T-r-o-u-b-l-e. Trouble. Oh Marylou, I think he is in a lot of trouble. Anyway, momma got all dressed up this morning. She looked gorgeous. She is getting off work early. She and Sam are coming to your house together. Will you please ask your momma to come see my surprise for momma?"

"Jasmine, momma already knows. She is coming. Now that you told me Sam was coming, I will call my brother, Shane, to invite him also. That will be so much fun. Does your momma know that you accepted the hope chest from Skyler's momma?"

"No, she doesn't know. She gave me until Monday to decide."

"Jasmine, my momma will have snacks also. It will be like a party."

"Great! Thank you. See you later."

Cashmere had a wonderful day at work. She

laughed, talked, and made a few incredible floral designs. Now she was on her way to her car to go home. Guess who she ran into. You guessed it, her ex-husband. This time he was alone. Boy did she feel energized. Since she had set her mind on not speaking, she walked right by him.

"Cashmere, why you look fantastic! What's going on?"

She paused, turned around and answered. "My life. Gotta run. I have a surprise party to go to this evening."

"I came back to apologize to you. There was no reason to snub you like I did. I wasn't sure how you were going to react when you saw me."

"That makes perfect sense. I accept your apology. I hope you have a good weekend. See you around."

Cashmere stood up tall, flipped her hair around, while walking gracefully to her car. As she unlocked the car door, her ex-husband ran up to her.

"Do you have someone new in your life?"

"Yes, I do. Me." Then she drove off.

Only two days earlier, she was a hot mess, shocked, ashamed, and miserable. Two days later, she was confident while holding to a made-up mind. She wished that she would have been able to video the look her ex-husband had on his face. In this situation, it was no need to fret about that because her brain indelibly recorded it. She glanced into her rear-view mirror, adjusting it to see if her ex was still there. He was standing behind her car, soaking up the fumes, as she sped off. Her adrenaline was pumping because she turned up the volume on her radio. Girl, what a difference two days made. She realized that attitude was everything. At that moment, she had a new one. That was the best feeling she had in a long time.

Cashmere did not need a song to come on the radio. She turned the radio off and started singing Patti Labelle's song, *I got a new attitude.* She pulled into her driveway. After parking, she strutted inside to freshen up before Sam came home. About the time she finished freshening up, she was still doing her happy dance routine when Sam walked in.

"Hey momma, "How was your day?"

"Sam, it was the best day ever. I will tell you all about it later. Let's go now. We don't want to be late."

Cashmere was beside herself. Missy, Kip, Marylou, Shane, and Jasmine were all standing around when Sam and Cashmere walked into the house.

Missy's decorations were cheerful looking along with the appetizing snacks. Sam had the selfie that they had taken earlier printed to symbolize their momma's new attitude. That photo was now a small banner. Everything was splendid. They all ate the snacks. Now it came to the time when Jasmine would present the surprise gift. The room was quiet.

Jasmine spoke, "Momma, Sam and I love you. I know this week was not your best week. We all know that grandmomma was very sick when you were a teenager. There were certain things that she could not do for you. She could not follow the tradition that all Southern girls looked forward to. That was a hope chest.

"Momma, although you do not have a lot of money, you gave me one of the best gifts I received ever, a hope chest, something that I would use on my journey to marriage. You took your creative talent and made me a special hope chest. I would not exchange it for the world. I like all the little details you created. Granted, you thought that I should accept Ms. Chadsworth's hope chest; but I could not bring myself to do it. I told you that I had made my decision and shared it with Skyler. He was extremely happy. Momma, I accepted the hope chest."

Jasmine's momma said, "I'm so happy that you did accept the chest. I feel good that you trusted that I wanted you to have it. And that you would not offend me."

She walked over to Jasmine and said, "Thank you

for that surprise. For your decision. So where is it?"

Jasmine showed her. "Here it is momma."

Cashmere looked.

"Why haven't you unwrapped it?"

"Momma because I wanted you to do me the honors."

"That's a switch. Sure, I will. You went all out to have a surprise. I want to help you all the way through it."

Sam brought the gift over to his momma. She started unwrapping it. As she continued, she marveled at its beauty. She ran her fingers over the details of the hope chest.

"My little girl. There is no way I could have afforded this. I am so happy you accepted it. It's truly magnificent."

"Momma, I have a few things in there already. Look in it and see. Sam drew his artistic interpretation of the three things that would make a difference in a husband and wife's relationship."

"Are you sure you want me to do this? You should be doing this."

"Please momma for me. Please, for me."

"Okay. Here is a box of white lace handkerchiefs. Nice. A pair of white gloves. I could use these. A pen-set, a journal, hmmm, a manila envelope which has writing on the outside in all caps: **DO NOT OPEN UNTIL A DATE IS SET**. Ok. I will not open it. That is probably really private. Oh, here is a card taped to the bottom of the chest."

"Read it momma."

"No. Are you sure? You don't have to show me everything that's in the chest."

"Yes, I am sure, momma. Please read it out loud for me. Please, momma."

"Ok. 'Dear Momma, this is my surprise gift for you. Now you have a hope chest. I have one too. Fill it up. Love Jasmine.'"

Cashmere cried like a baby. "No! No! Jasmine. I cain't accept this. I cain't…"

"Momma, I told you I would never trade my hope chest for something else. I meant it. This is for you. I kept my word to decide before Monday."

Cashmere asked, "What did Skyler say?"

"He was happy that I accepted the gift. His momma shipped it out the same day. She was happy too. So, when I told you I had decided what to do, I could not tell you because this is the reason. I wanted to give it to you. Momma, I told Skyler I will fill him in later on the details."

"My little lady. Your generosity is overwhelming. I would not have guessed this in a million years. I guess I must accept your gift because I really wanted you to accept her gift.

"Momma, accepting a gift is a sign of humility."

"Thank you. Lesson learned. What a twist. What a twist. When are you going to tell Skyler, what happened?"

"I'm going to call him when I get home."

"Ok, then Jasmine, let's go. Thank you all for

hosting this surprise for me. I will never ever forget it. My daughter discerned that I would really appreciate it. We are leaving now. I have to go. We will see you all later. What a wonderful day this has been."

On the way home, Sam was very generous in his compliments to his momma and Jasmine. He said, "Momma, when I get married, I want to have a wife that has your qualities. Momma, you love hard. You are also patient. You tried your best to communicate with daddy. Even though daddy left us, you did not. That shows me you value marriage and family. You never gave up trying. You are loyal. You stayed with us. Without a doubt, you are taking good care of us. I know that it is hard. Thank you so much."

Cashmere smiled and said, "Thank you Sam for noticing and for always trying to encourage me."

Sam expressed his feeling to Jasmine.

"Jasmine you actually know how to share. In other words, you are not selfish. Do you know how many young teens would have opted to keep that beautiful chest, take pictures of it, and post it on social media? You taught me that sacrifice is not really a sacrifice when you love someone. I can see where I can make changes in preparation for my marriage one day. You are a strong person…a doer."

Jasmine said, "Sam, thank you so much. That means a lot."

Cashmere said, "I know these last two years have not been easy. But I'm looking forward to making the best of my situation."

Jasmine commented, "That's good momma. Thanks, big brother. I hope I can continue to be positive for you as well as momma. And you all have been there for me too. Thank you."

They were at home in no time. Jasmine quickly ran to her room to call Skyler. He answered the telephone promptly.

"Hey Jasmine, so what happened?"

"Skyler, it was unbelievable! We gave momma a

surprise party.

"Why did you give her a surprise party? Was it her birthday?"

"No. You see, my momma never had a hope chest because her momma was sickly. She could not do a lot of things for her. Later, when I called to say I wanted the hope chest, I was going to make it a gift for momma."

"Jasmine, that is incredibly noble. My mother is really going to be happy."

"Skyler, momma was concerned about what you would think. That makes me feel so much better. It was remarkable. I asked momma to unwrap it for me. Then, I asked her to look at the items in there. She said I could use the white gloves. When she found out it was for her, she cried so hard."

"Was that a good cry or bad cry?"

"It was a good cry. Thank you so very much. Please thank Mrs. Chadsworth for me. Momma would have never been able to give me such an expensive gift; furthermore, I would not have been able to give her one either. You two made it possible for my momma to have her own hope chest. I gotta go; but I wanted you to have the details."

"I'm happy about that. Thank you so much for calling. I will share that with my momma."

After Jasmine hung up, she went ahead to tell her momma what Skyler said. Cashmere was so pleased. Not only that, she had already found a place for the hope chest in her bedroom. Sam happened to remember to ask Cashmere how her day was again. When she told them what their daddy did, they laughed.

"See momma. You still got it."

Cashmere said, "Yes, today was a good day. A very, very good day. Your daddy got a chance to see me at my best, which has been a long time since that has happened. It felt so good. He even asked me if I had someone new in my life."

Jasmine burst out, "What did you say?"

"I said yes. Me."

Sam said, "Momma I have to admit that was a good one."

"Jasmine, I want you to know this. Sam, I want you to learn from this statement. They always come back. Many times, not for a good motive."

"What do you mean by that momma?" Jasmine asked.

"Kids within two days after seeing how your daddy treated me, I had made up my mind to go on with my life. I stopped mourning in a sense about our relationship when I got up, did my hair, nails and focused on a new life. When your daddy came by, I was not sure of his intentions. He said it was to apologize to me. Clearly, I got to see that my change in attitude along with my appearance made him curious. He wanted to come back.

"His curiosity showed me a lot. First of all, I reasoned that he had the potential to interrupt the little progress I had made. Next, I thought about this if he left once, he could do it again. Most of all, he was prepared to cheat on that woman who he was with two days ago. I think that the possibility of a happy reunion was not based upon love, but lust. How could that last?

"Remember, it was written that a man and a woman should leave their parents and become one flesh. Although, I had been hoping for a reconciliation with your daddy, I saw that I needed to move on when I saw him the second time. I could be wrong. But it appeared that he was up to no good. I hope I am mistaken.

"Let's get ready for bed. I want to take you out for breakfast tomorrow morning. We have had enough grilled cheese and baloney sandwiches this week."

Cashmere was not looking at the windstorm any longer. It was about change, positive behavior and being a strong example for herself along with her children. Through her challenges, she wanted them to grasp that adversity was an opportunity to develop integrity, mental strength and to become a well-rounded person with unlimited potential.

Chapter 8

The community college that Marylou and River attended sponsored a talent show; while the coordinators of the event encouraged students who had a talent to sign up. Marylou knew that this would be terrific entertainment for her momma. It would be like a girls' night out.

The talent show would start at seven in the evening and would end eight thirty p.m. The line up on the program included singers, dancers and musicians taking part. Since Marylou did not know many of the students, this would give her an opportunity to hopefully meet some and learn what campus night life was like.

The first person who opened the show sang, *Sweet Home Alabama.*

It was not the best rendition, but everyone clapped. The next act was a person playing the piano. It was brilliant, but awfully sad. The program was a little hum drum. About an hour had passed when Marylou asked her momma if she would like something to eat. It was less than thirty minutes left in the program, so her momma said, "No I can wait."

Right after she said that someone dimmed the lights. The person on stage wore a knee-length trench coat and a hat. Then the MC said, "It looks like we have Bruno Mars with us tonight."

Marylou sat up. She moaned, "No-o-o! It cain't be."

Her mother touched her, "Honey are you all right?"

"Momma I think that is River."

Mrs. Marshall replied, "River? The nice young man that called you one evening?"

"I think so momma."

The next thing they saw was the person on stage had taken off the trench coat. He had on a white t-shirt with a pair of loose slacks. He began with a simple ballet move when he ran across the stage. Then he slid to the front of the stage on his knees, stood up and broke into a serious Bruno Mars dance move. The crowd jumped out of their seats, and it sounded like it thundered. The women in the auditorium started screaming. Not only that, Mrs. Marshall jumped up too, screaming as loud as she could. Marylou bowed her head.

Mrs. Marshall tried to get Marylou to stand up. Someone started a chant that said, "Go River. Go River. Go River. Go River."

Marylou could not believe it. It was her momma who had started the chant. Because of her rhythmic chant, the lights came up and a spotlight went to Missy. That is when River noticed Marylou. He got terribly excited. He took his hat off, threw it to Mrs.

Marshall. Marylou ran out. She learned that night at the talent show this fact: River was not lying when he told her he liked to dance and sing Bruno Mars songs. Mrs. Marshall stayed in the auditorium for the entire show. Marylou never returned. She sat in the lobby. When the show was over, Mrs. Marshall went out to find Marylou sitting in a corner. She asked, "Are you feeling ok sweetie?"

"Momma why did you do that?"

"Do what?"

Marylou said, "You started singing 'Go River.'"

"Darling, you have a lot to learn. I am only thirty-nine years old. I love life. I love having fun. How would you have felt if no one cheered you on with a song like that? He was really good. I hate you missed it. You have to learn to enjoy life. Not to be so stuck up. I had fun. Thank you for inviting me. I have not had this kind of fun in a long time. I have been missing out."

Not long after she said that River walked out. Mrs.

Marshall said, "River, I'm Marylou's momma. You did such a great job on your dance routine. I'm genuinely happy that my daughter invited me."

"Thank you, Mrs. Marshall. Did you like my routine Marylou?"

"Marylou sadly said, "I didn't stay to see it all."

River asked, "Are you feeling ok?"

Marylou whimpered, "River I was ashamed; but my momma enjoyed it. I'm sorry."

River's heartbreaking response was, "I wish that you were not ashamed of me. I'm not ashamed of you."

Marylou trembled. "Yes, I'm sorry. I was acting like a rotten child. Please accept my apology. I was surprised. I promise that I will never do that again."

"Well, since you promised, I forgive you. Also Mrs. Marshall, thank you very much for your support. You got the crowd going. I was a little nervous because a lot of the students are older than I am. When I heard your distinctive voice, I grew more confident."

"River, you are talented. We look forward to seeing you perform again. Have a good night."

"Good night Mrs. Marshall. Good night, Marylou."

Mrs. Marshall asked, "River are you here alone?"

"No, Mrs. Marshall. My parents are here. They helped put the talent show together for the students. My momma teaches music. My dad teaches dance here at the community college. Would you like to meet them?"

"Sure, I would." Mrs. Marshall replied.

"I will be right back."

River came right back with his parents. "Mrs. Marshall, here are my parents."

"Pleased to meet you Mr. & Mrs. Parish. My name is Missy Marshall. River said that you planned the entire talent show."

"Yes, we did. And it was such a success. We were going out to get a light snack. Would you like to join us?" River and Marylou looked at each other.

"River said, "Mrs. Marshall, Marylou is not sixteen years old yet."

Mrs. Marshall teased him. "That's true River. The date is not with you and Marylou. The date is between me and your parents. You two would be coming along. It would be good to talk with them about our wishes when she turns sixteen. Would that be ok?"

They all went to the small café for a bite to eat. That tickled the two young teens. They looked at it like it was a date because the chaperon had to be her parents or brother.

During their conversation at the café, River's parents expressed the same feeling that Marylou's parents had. In other words, all the parents agreed that they should have a chaperon. That may have appeared old fashioned to some teens to have a parent or an older brother as a chaperone. To them, it was not old fashioned. They had the same view on having a chaperon. They wanted to remain virgins until they married each other, or if they married someone else.

They knew that if they did not keep their virginity, they could rob their future spouse of a pure, clean union in marriage. That was remarkable that they were all in agreement.

Chapter 9

It was Monday morning. Although it was school as usual for Jasmine, coupled with basketball practice right after her last class, today though, was a little bit different. The Coach announced to the team that he might be getting a new assistant, and in any event, he would know for sure on Tuesday. Then he could let everyone know.

Jasmine wondered if that announcement had anything to do with the conversation that this girl had with Tommy last week. First of all, the team practiced hard without Tommy. After they finished practice, Jasmine went into the locker room to get her hoodie. When she came out Tommy was there waiting on her.

"Tommy, I thought that you were not going to be here today. Coach Van Damme announced that at the beginning of practice. He said that there might be a new assistant coming to help him. What is going on? Are you all right?"

"Jasmine, I wanted to tell you right away what was happening with me. I couldn't wait."

"What is it?"

"When I was twelve years old, the girl you saw last week and I, made a pact that we would get married when we were eighteen years old. I am six feet three inches tall. I am only sixteen years old. She is eighteen years old now. Because of my height, people have always thought I was older.

"You know some people in the South get married really young. They think something is wrong with you if you do not do the same. In my case, her parents started planning that we would get married. I did not think much about it. It is like when your parents tell you that you should be a lawyer or something else, they think you should do, but you do not seriously think about it until you have had a little more exposure and then it changes. Her parents got married young. She told them about our agreement. Even as you saw her talking to me, she was pressuring me to marry her. I told her …I did not know her like that. By that I meant, we were kids. She was trying to hold me to that pact. When I talked with my parents, they said that she was being silly. My parents went to talk with her parents about that subject. In fact, trying to talk or reason with her parents was just like talking to children.

"Her parents are trying to make trouble for me since they believe that a promise to marry should be honored, no matter what age. That girl who you saw said that if I didn't marry her, she would make something up about me."

"Oh, my goodness Tommy. How are you all going to handle that?"

"My parents had already been working on an

opportunity for me to be an exchange student in Europe. With a few more phone calls, they arranged for it to happen sooner."

"How soon?"

"I will be leaving on Saturday Jasmine."

"Saturday? How long will you be there?"

"Until I finish college?"

"Oh no Tommy! Why so long?"

"My parents think that this is a good program. I could not afford the potential distractions or accusations."

"Well, it sounds like you are running away."

"It sounds like that, but eventually, I was going to go to school in Europe. We can still keep in contact."

"How? Will you still be able to help me with my drills?"

"No Jasmine. You know that. We can communicate from time to time via skype or zoom."

"I guess you have to do what you have to do and what your parents say do. That is how that girl's parents thought. I do not believe this. I do not like it. I know that is selfish. That is how I feel. I know you will do well. I'll try my best to be happy for you."

"Thank you, Jasmine. It will pass before you know it. You are busy anyway. Then you will probably get a scholarship to play basketball in college. I wanted you to hear it from me, not through my uncle. I am sorry, as you can see. We will see each other again."

"Yes Tommy. You are right. At least I have the rest of the week to see you."

"Not really Jasmine. I'm going to visit my grandparents tomorrow in Atlanta. I will leave for Europe from there. That's why I needed to see you today."

Jasmine started crying. "I know we have not known each other long. I appreciated the encouragement that you gave me. Your comments kept me going. I am going to miss you. I hope we can stay connected. I have to go now because my momma asked me to pick up an item from the store.

So, I just wish you didn't have to go so soon or for that matter not go at all."

"I know we haven't known each other long. I cain't afford to stay here. You can still message me about your progress on the drills." They hugged each other. Jasmine left with tears running down her cheeks.

When Jasmine got home, she heard her momma in the kitchen humming out a song. Her mother loved R&B music. Jasmine had heard this song several times. She really wanted to watch her momma sing with the broom handle; otherwise, she would have joined her. Her momma had a very soulful voice. The song was by Luther Vandross. It was *A House is Not a Home.* Jasmine paid close attention to her momma. Her momma had not sung out like that in a long time. The words were fresh in her mind. She hummed the musical prelude rendition of the song, then began singing the solo and chorus part of the song once she gained momentum.

Jasmine watched as her momma hummed out the lyrics that she did not know. Later she continued with the lyrics that she knew. Her momma was feeling it deep, deep down in her soul. She started singing again.

Jasmine yelled out, "Momma I'm here. Yes, momma I heard the words to that song. That was pretty good. I see why you sent me to the dollar store to pick up another broom. You have worn that broom out." They both laughed. Momma you should sing out loud more often. You sounded extremely good."

"Thanks Baby. How was your day?"

"Not good. Tommy is moving to Europe to be a part of an exchange program until he finishes college."

"Are you ok baby girl?"

"No mam. I'm sad. A little angry. Been crying. It is certainly not fair. This girl in his hometown, in a sense, is the cause. She wants Tommy to marry her."

"Marry her?"

"Yes. She and Tommy agreed when he was twelve years old that they would get married at eighteen years old. She is eighteen and he is sixteen. Both are not eighteen. So, he was accepted into an exchange program; therefore, his parents were able to get him in sooner because she had threatened to make trouble for him."

"Seems like it was a good idea to get him out of that situation. Spiteful people can ruin your life forever sweetheart."

"Well momma, tomorrow he leaves for Atlanta to visit with his grandparents. Then off to Europe."

"Let's sit down and have a cup of tea. You can tell me all about it."

"Okay momma. I'm just so surprised."

Cashmere turned on the stove to heat the water in the teapot. Then she got two cups from the cupboard. Jasmine got a couple of flavors of tea bags, sugar, lemon and placed them on the table. Then she went back to get the spoons. After they prepared their tea, Cashmere comforted her daughter by saying, "Jasmine, I'm sure everything will turn out well with Tommy. He will keep in contact. You know he will have an adjustment period when he gets to Europe. In that case, give him a little time. You know Skyler loves basketball. Maybe you two can talk about the drills they run in Sarasota-Bradenton. I have always heard that Florida produced excellent athletes."

"That's a good idea momma. I will keep that in mind. I do not even think I have told Skyler that Tommy was helping me with drills. Yeah, I'll do that."

"I talked to Missy today. She stopped by the shop to pick up some flowers. She told me that she and Marylou went to a talent show last night. They had a lot of fun."

"Hmm...Marylou didn't mention it."

"It was a girls' night out with the two of them. Maybe we can have a girls' night out."

"What would you do momma?"

"Hmmm, I don't know. What would you like?"

"You know what I would like. I want to see basketball.

"I got a better idea. Why don't we play a game of one-on-one? I used to play with my brothers and my cousin until they outgrew me. You can go easy on your momma."

"You never told me that Momma."

"I could use a little exercise. Let's go to the Clausell Community Center. I have not been down there in years. What about that?"

Jasmine giggled, "Momma can you really play?"

"How tall are you Jasmine?"

"I'm five feet eleven inches."

"We are almost the same height. Then, it will be an even game."

"I don't know momma."

"If it starts getting rough on you, we can stop."

"Rough on me? Yes, I have height and weight on

my side, and a little experience."

"Ok momma, well, let's go down to Clausell Community Center early Saturday morning."

"That's good Jasmine. What about nine in the morning?"

"Ok Momma, we would need a pre-game meal about six in the morning."

"Well let's say we play ten in the morning and eat at seven."

"That'll work momma."

"What does a pre-game meal consist of Jasmine?"

"Some protein, carbohydrates, and fruit."

"Ok. What about baked chicken, brown rice, sautéed kale, and a small fruit smoothie?

"That sounds good momma. That's a lot to cook Saturday morning."

"I will make this for dinner Friday night, and we can have leftovers Saturday morning. All I would have to do is make a fruit smoothie."

"That's great momma. I'm really excited because

we don't have practice on Friday."

"Well, no excuses. Let the game begin on Saturday morning at ten."

About ten Friday night, before the game between Cashmere and Jasmine on Saturday morning, Coach Van Damme called to inform Jasmine that he was going to host a picnic for the team. He asked Cashmere if Jasmine could attend the little get-together for his team at the Clausell Community Center at noon on Saturday.

Cashmere mentioned to Jasmine's basketball coach that they were going to be at the park at ten. As far as she knew, Jasmine could attend. He explained that time had gotten away from him and apologized for calling so late. He also invited Cashmere to come if she wanted to attend. Since Jasmine was already asleep, Cashmere did not wake her up.

Chapter 10

The next morning, Cashmere got up about six thirty to prepare breakfast for the two and to make the fruit smoothie. When Jasmine got up, she went straight to the bathroom to freshen up for breakfast. As she was about finished dressing, her momma called out, "Breakfast is ready."

Jasmine strolled into the kitchen with a certain confidence. "Good morning momma. Today is the day, we see who gets the trophy."

Cashmere joked, "I wonder who you got your bravado from?"

Jasmine burst into laughter. "It's natural. I am hyped momma! We have never done this before."

"Well, save some of your energy. Your coach

called last night after you had gone to bed. He decided to have a picnic for the team today at noon. I told him we were going to be there at ten. And that you would be able to come."

"Yeah, that's great! I can introduce you to my teammates and coach. You can come too momma."

"That's right. Your coach invited me to attend."

"Good. Let's eat!"

After they finished eating, they cleaned the kitchen and packed some extra clothes to change into for the picnic. Jasmine also brought a basketball in case there was not one available. They made it to the center a little bit before ten a.m.

Cashmere found a court that no one was playing on, so that is why they parked the car at that court. They claimed the court right away and started warming up. Jasmine had such excitement brewing in her until she could hardly contain herself. You see her daddy had never played a game of one-on-one basketball with her. That interaction with her momma was what Jasmine needed.

Initially, each of them shot a few baskets. What was going to make this game interesting was that not only was Jasmine left-handed, Cashmere was also left-handed too. Jasmine was running around the court like a jack rabbit, all excited. This is what happened during the warmup. Cashmere couldn't wait until Jasmine would throw the ball to her to shoot. She did not run up and down the court. She shot the ball wherever she was. It was clear that Cashmere was managing her energy level pretty well, waiting to unleash what energy she had during the game. This warm-up took about thirty minutes.

Then Jasmine said, "Momma why don't you take the ball out first, since I have a little edge over you. Cashmere took possession of the ball to start the game. As she was coming up the court, Jasmine started to guard her. When Cashmere went to the left, Jasmine went to the left. When Cashmere approached the hoop, so did Jasmine. Then there was light for Cashmere. Two points.

"Nice momma. Keep it up."

When Jasmine took the ball out, the breakfast that Cashmere had eaten took possession of her body. Following that burst of energy from the food, she used every bit of her energy to jump high. Cashmere solved the problem of guarding Jasmine by blocking her shot. Cashmere got the ball and went for a smooth layup. Two points for Cashmere. Then there was darkness for Jasmine. Now Cashmere had four points. Jasmine took the ball out and brought it back in. As she was dribbling the ball down the court, she got faster and faster as she made her way to the side for a three-point bucket. And she made it. Three points for Jasmine.

When she made the shot, she taunted her momma and said, "Momma that is the shot, Skyler saw me make. He said it was beautiful and I was too." Cashmere was laughing and praying at the same time, as she watched her little girl really get into her game.

The end of the game would be twenty-one points and whoever got there first was the winner. Four points for Cashmere. Three points for Jasmine. Earlier they had talked about each having two-time outs, just to get a break, especially if the run was too hard for either of them. Certainly, no one would foul the other, you would think.

It was Cashmere's turn to take the ball out. She was bringing the ball up court. Jasmine was guarding her momma a little closer. And wouldn't you know it, Cashmere who was left-handed, went to make a lay-up with her right hand and Jasmine slapped her on the arm.

"Foul!"

"I'm sorry momma. Did that hurt?"

"It hurt you because I'm going to the free throw line. I'm going to take my time to shoot that basketball to get those two points."

Cashmere made the two points. Now, the score was six points and Jasmine had three points. Jasmine realized then and only then that her momma had some skills. She knew she had to tie the score as soon as possible. When she brought the ball in, she decided to go up for a lay-up, making it. Now the score was six points for Cashmere, five points for Jasmine.

Afterwards, Cashmere took the ball out and brought it in to make the three-point shot. The score was nine points for Cashmere. Five points for Jasmine. Jasmine looked compassionately at her momma, shook her head and asked, "Momma do you need a break? We have been running a little hard."

"No Jasmine. Do you need a break?"

Jasmine could not believe that her thirty-six-year-old momma, mother of two teenagers, was hanging in there with her fifteen-year-old daughter, toe to toe. More than that she was not breathing hard. Jasmine attributed her momma's not breathing hard to the strength she had for singing, being that Cashmere could hold a note for a long time. As Jasmine was contemplating her next shot, she realized that playing against her momma was not as easy as she had thought it would be. Jasmine said to herself, "Momma is five feet ten inches tall with catlike quickness and deceptive speed all bound up in a well-developed muscular body that could jump out of the gym."

Cashmere had a flashback of a few old memories about how it was when she played ball with her cousin and older brothers. At that precise moment, her recall allowed her to steal the ball from Jasmine, run down the court and make a layup. Two points. Cashmere now had eleven points. Jasmine had five points.

Cashmere called, "Time out." Jasmine was serious. She did not like for one moment that her momma stole the ball from her. Anyway, they got a little Gatorade to drink and sat down on the court. They did not want to take the chance of leaving the court for one minute for fear that someone could jump on the court and take it.

Surely now, Jasmine had a different level of respect

for her momma. She asked, "Momma did you ever want to play basketball in high school and go to college to play?"

Cashmere answered, "Jasmine I loved basketball. I played at home and at school, but not on an organized team. Your granddaddy thought that playing ball was not for girls. Even though, I knew I would do well, he only allowed me to do things that girls do, like participating in a pageant or being a cheerleader."

"I'm extremely sorry momma that it was like that for you. As I can tell, I guess you kept your talent a secret."

"Oh, I knew I had a talent. The coach knew I had a talent. Even my daddy knew I had a talent. He could not understand that many girls have a desire to play sports. He told me that he feared that some of the girls would try to hurt me. Jasmine I never thought about the fact that guys that play sports tried to hurt the opponent, so what would be the difference with girls? Possibly naïve on my part. I thought he held on to old school thinking, which caused a measure of embarrassment because I longed to play the sport. My only option was to get married and raise a family."

"Has it been painful for you to watch me play when you couldn't play?"

"No dear. It has been invigorating for me. At first, I thought that you would follow my path and get married. But I see your goal is to focus on basketball first and marriage later. That is ok with me. Remember though, your goals should make you happy and it should be for you, not for me. So, let's get back on the court before I get too stiff. It's your turn to take the ball out Jasmine."

Jasmine brought the ball in and made an unbelievable three-point bucket. The score was eleven points for Cashmere and eight points for Jasmine. Cashmere smiled. Then someone called out, "Jasmine!" She turned around and dropped the ball. Her momma asked, "What is it, Jasmine? Who is it that said your name? There are too many people here."

Jasmine answered, "Momma this is Tommy. Tommy is who called my name."

Tommy said, "Jasmine that was a great shot!"

She asked, "Why are you here? I thought your flight left today."

"It does. My uncle knew I did not get a chance to say goodbye to the team. In that case, he thought it would be encouraging to the team to have a picnic to say goodbye and take a later flight today. My parents agreed."

"Oh Tommy. I am extremely happy you came back. This is my momma, Cashmere Summers."

"Hi Ms. Summers. I see where your daughter got her basketball talent. So Jasmine is not going to need my help to run drills. You can help her. It would be so motivating for her."

Coach Van Damme came over to investigate the situation. "Jasmine who is this person giving you a run for your money?"

"Hi Coach. This is my momma, Cashmere Summers."

"Mrs. Summers, were you the one I talked to last night?"

"I'm the one. I am Ms. Summers. My daughter and I had this outing planned a few days ago. So nice to meet you."

"You too. I would like to talk with you later about helping the girls maybe once a week if you have the circumstances."

"Coach, we can talk about it later."

"I know we interrupted your game, but I think it's time for both of you to take a time out to come spend some time with Tommy before he leaves for Europe."

"That's ok with me if that is ok with momma.

"Yes, that is good. We can meet you at the picnic once we change our clothes."

Jasmine and her momma got their clothes from the car and headed to the shower. Cashmere commented,

"Jasmine that was so nice of your coach to have a going away picnic for Tommy. You never told me what Tommy looked like. You only spoke about his height."

"What do you mean? Who does he look like? Like momma, he looks Irish. He has reddish blonde hair and blue eyes or in straightforward terms, he is white. Momma, you know that doesn't matter to me."

"It doesn't matter to me either. However, to some people it matters."

"Well, you know momma, it shouldn't matter anyway. He is leaving tonight for at least three to four years."

"Yeah, what if he comes back to Monroeville?"

Jasmine replied, "He may come back. But that doesn't mean that I will be here or that we would be a couple."

"Okay. Okay. Let's go enjoy the picnic."

When they got to the picnic, Jasmine introduced her momma to all of her teammates. Then she excused herself to go over to talk with Tommy. Coach Van Damme seized the opportunity to talk with Cashmere. He told her that he and Tommy had watched the last part of their warm-up and the game. He asked her to consider volunteering her time to help the girls one day a week or maybe to volunteer to be a chaperone for the girls when they went to other schools to play.

Cashmere wanted to talk to Jasmine about it before she considered his proposal to see how she would feel about it. The coach thought that it was a good idea to do that. They could talk about it later. He was really impressed with Cashmere.

Although, he agreed that it would be a good idea to talk to Jasmine about Cashmere volunteering, he knew that would really encourage the team. With that, he said to himself, 'That Cashmere is so fine with those killer moves, I must find out more about her."

He asked, "Mrs. Summers, how long have you been playing basketball?"

Cashmere responded, "I have been playing basketball since I was a little girl. By the way it's Ms. Summers."

"Ms. Summers, would it be safe to say Jasmine got her talent from you?"

"I think that is safe to say. My ex-husband wasn't interested in sports after he injured himself."

"How sad. When was the last time you played a game of basketball?"

"That's a good question. The last time I played, I was a junior in high school."

"Why did you stop playing?"

"My daddy didn't think it was ladylike. Since my daddy did not want me to play, I sort of let it go. I went ahead, got married, and had two children, Sam, who is seventeen and Jasmine who is fifteen."

"Does Sam like basketball?"

"Sam is still trying to find out what he wants to do. Jasmine has the passion that I had when I was younger. I have been divorced about two years. First of all, I think it would be good for Jasmine and me if I volunteered. I know it would encourage Sam too. What about you? How did you come to Monroeville to become a coach?"

"My brother and I came to the University of Alabama on a basketball scholarship. He came first. I followed two years later. After he graduated, he accepted a job at Georgia Mesona in Perdue, Alabama. When I graduated, my dad suggested that I look for a job near my brother. So, in short, the only job I could find was a coaching job at Monroe County High School. I really liked it and that is why I have been here fifteen years."

"So, Coach Van Damme, do you live in Monroeville?"

"Yes, I do. Not too far from the high school."

"Do you have other family? Cashmere asked.

"No, it's me. No children. No spouse."

"Where are you originally from?"

"I'm from Tuscaloosa. My parents are from

Ireland."

"That's interesting. You do not have a strong accent. Anyway, my daughter is very happy you are coaching here."

The picnic was so delightful for everyone. Jasmine got a chance to spend time with Tommy. Coach got a chance to spend time with Cashmere. And Tommy left with wonderful memories.

On the way home, Cashmere, thanked Jasmine for a beautiful day. She informed Jasmine that Coach Van Damme wanted her to consider volunteering to help the team.

"How do you feel about that Jasmine?"

"Momma I think that would be great! Would you come every day?"

"No, one day per week or I could volunteer to be a chaperone for the team."

"Why don't you do both momma? I would really like it. That might also get Sam interested in my game."

"I think so too Jasmine."

"Let's see what Sam thinks. He should be at home when we get there."

"Momma, Sam's here."

Jasmine jumped out of the car.

"Sam! Sam! Coach Van Damme asked momma to volunteer one day per week with my team. Isn't that great?"

"Yeah. Momma do you even like basketball?"

"Yes son. I do. I used to play before I got married."

"Well, that is fantastic Momma. I gotta come out and watch you play. I might even start playing again."

Then Sam started laughing. "When are you going to start volunteering?

"Well, once we work out the schedule."

Sam was cheerful. "Ok Momma. You are really serious. Happy to see you start to live again. Call him now before it is too late. Don't want him to get someone else."

"Jasmine, do you have his telephone number?"

"Here it is momma. Do you really want to do it? It could be really hard work."

"I'm sure if you are?

"I'm sure momma."

Cashmere dialed his number.

"Hey, this is Cashmere Summers."

"I know who it is. I would know your voice anywhere. Did you check with your children about volunteering?"

"Yes. I did check with them. I think it is good news. Jasmine and Sam are excited about me volunteering to work with the team. Sam even expressed that he might start coming to watch Jasmine practice."

"That seems like a win-win Ms. Summers. So, if you have time on Monday, can you stop by the school's gym to watch practice. In a few days, we can work out your schedule."

"Ok, I can be there around four thirty p.m. I may

be able to convince Sam to come also."

Although that was a good move for the Coach to have Cashmere work as a volunteer, there was yet a lot to see how it would work out.

Chapter 11

Coach had organized a great send off for Tommy. The girls' basketball team had a chance to spend time with Tommy, who had encouraged them to continue to practice hard and never quit. Now they would have the momma of one of the basketball players, who had played the game for years, to help them out.

Cashmere Summers was as excited about changing her life as the girls were to have her on their team. She showed up about four thirty p.m. as she had said. She asked Sam to meet her there. They studied a few of the drills that the girls were doing. They noticed that all of the girls were involved except one.

Sam said, She must be on the injured list.

Cashmere agreed with Sam. They waved to Jasmine, trying to signal that they would wait for her at the car. Ms. Summers approached Coach to thank him for inviting her to watch the girls' practice. After he ended practice, the girl on the sideline did not leave with all of the other girls. She walked over to Coach Van Damme and quietly spoke with him. Also, he talked to her in the same manner, then scooted away after she left the building.

The next day she came back to practice, but she did not practice. Sam observed her as she watched the practice again, then walked over to sit with her. "I saw you yesterday. Are you on the team?"

"No, I'm not. I simply came to watch."

"So, did I. I am not a big basketball fan; but my mother asked me if I would like to come with her to look at my sister practice and so I did. My name is Sam Summers."

"My name is Malinda Fox."

"It's good to meet you, Malinda."

"Are you going to come to watch them practice tomorrow?"

"Yes, I think I am."

"Ok, I will see you tomorrow."

Malinda appeared pleasant as she walked over to Coach Van Damme again. He seemed uninterested in what she had to say; although, he talked briefly to her and left the building.

Jasmine walked over to Sam. "How do you think I did in practice today?"

Sam replied, "I think you did okay."

Jasmine added, "I saw you talking to a girl in the bleachers. Who is she?"

"Her name is Malinda. She was merely hanging out watching practice. I think she wants to be on the team. She said she was coming back tomorrow. I told her I was too. I'm surprised you don't know her."

Jasmine claimed, "Different people have come to watch us at times, but not every day. Maybe you are right about that. I could not get a good look at her because she had on a baseball cap with sunglasses. Well big brother if that will keep you coming every day to see me practice. That's ok."

Malinda visited every day of that week; but unlike the first three days, she did not go up to talk with Coach Van Damme. The reason could be that on Thursday, Ms. Summers came to watch the practice and he was busy with her, trying to complete her volunteer schedule. Thursday afternoon she would help with drills and on Friday night she would chaperone all away games.

The following week Malinda showed up again. This time she went up to Coach Van Damme after practice was over and yelled at him. He told her she could no longer watch the girls' practice. Sam followed her after she stormed out of the building.

"Are you okay Malinda?"

"I'm annoyed that the Coach has asked me to stop coming to watch the girls' practice."

"Why do you think he did that?"

"I asked him a question that he refuses to answer."

"If you do not mind, please tell me what you asked him? Maybe, I can help you."

"I don't think you can help me. You wouldn't know."

"Try me. If I do not know the answer, I will buy you ice cream. If I get the answer, you can buy me ice cream."

She gave him a half-cocked smile, "Okay."

"Okay, what did you ask him?"

"I asked him where Tommy was?"

"That's easy. Tommy moved to Europe."

She laughed, "That is really funny. It looks like you would do anything to get ice cream."

"I'm not joking. He left Saturday. The girls' team had a picnic for him. I was there."

Malinda looked at Sam, dropped her bag, dropped to her knees and screamed, "We were supposed to get married! He did not even tell me goodbye. Please do not tell anyone that you told me that."

"I'm so sorry Malinda. You don't have to buy me the ice cream today, but tomorrow for sure."

"I was so sure that he would marry me. I am so embarrassed. My parents are going to look at me as a failure."

"A failure? Why? Tommy was only sixteen years old. How old are you?"

"I'm eighteen years old."

Sam moved in to say, "I will be eighteen in a few months. Maybe we can hang out until you feel better."

"I don't know. I am so confused. What am I going to tell my parents?"

"Tell them the truth. Tell them he was too young to get married. Tell them that you are too young to get married. Stand firm on this. Then, they will believe you."

"Well maybe you can come with me while I tell them."

"Sure. I will Malinda."

"Thank you, Sam. I need help. My parents have put a lot of pressure on me."

"You're welcome. You have nothing to be ashamed of. What kind of things do you like to do?"

Malinda said, "I really like to ride my bike."

Sam admitted, "I did too until someone stole my bike."

Malinda asked, "What else do you like to do."

Sam said, "I like to paint more than I like to draw."

Malinda said, "I like to draw more than paint."

Sam had changed Malinda's depressed feeling around by talking about something she enjoyed. Sam said, "I will paint a sunset and you can draw a portrait. There is an art store not very far away. Is it a possibility that we can go there?"

"Yes, that's a possibility."

"Once you tell your parents, you can get that Tommy problem behind you. After you settle that with your parents, let's go to the art store. Oh,

Malinda that does not mean that I have forgotten the ice cream."

"We can tell your parents this weekend. What day is good for you?"

"Today. Sam, thank you for wanting to help me do this; nevertheless, I must do it by myself, by standing firm like you said and being courageous. Yes, today is the day before I overthink it and not do it."

"I must say that I admire you going right ahead to settle this with your parents. Did you really want to marry Tommy?"

"Let me put it this way. As I said earlier, I got a lot of pressure from my parents and more than marriage, I wanted to please them. I am confused and I have a lot to sort out. So, I'll see you around."

"Hey Malinda, please take my number. If you need moral support, please give me a quick call or text."

She took his number. Malinda confessed, "I cain't promise that I will call you right away. Please, be patient."

With a sad face, Malinda waved goodbye to Sam. Once she arrived home, she found both of her parents sitting at the dining room table. They asked, "Did you find out where Tommy was hiding?"

"Yes, I did, momma and daddy. He has gone to Europe. And he is not coming back. I am happy that he left because I would have married him to please you. It would have been a shotgun wedding without the baby. I am glad he left. He did not love me. What kind of marriage would that have been? He could not love me the way I needed. I would have married someone that you made me terrorize. Surely, now I am not going to get married to Tommy. You can say whatever you want to say about me. I am not going to let it affect me anymore.

"Because you two fell in love, married at a young age, doing whatever else you did, does not mean that it should happen for me, or for that matter that I want it to happen to me. May I get a truthful answer to these questions? Are you two happily in love? Or did you settle for each other like your parents did? If so, I cannot. I'm sorry that I have disappointed you."

Malinda's daddy said, "Honey you have not disappointed me. I needed to hear you out. At most, I felt that if it was good enough for your momma and me to get married young, it was good enough for you. I am sorry that we put pressure on you. As far as those questions that you asked, here is the answer. I loved your momma. Yes, it was pressure. I'm happy now, but it took a while to get there."

Malinda's momma stated, "Thank you for respectfully sharing your feelings. We have feelings too. But currently, your feelings are more important. Never would I want you to go about marriage like I did. Honestly, I do not think that I would have gotten it if you did not tell me the truth. Those two questions you asked us made my heart silently ache. I do love your daddy. I can say that neither one of us showed a sweet love to you. For this I am sorry. Thank you for letting us know."

Malinda responded to her parents by hugging them while telling them that she would like to go to art school. She would like to get married one day, but not right away. Since Sam gave Malinda good advice about telling her parents the truth, no doubt it affected her parents' thoughts and actions as well as motivated Malinda to do something that she loved doing.

Malinda told her parents that she wanted to go to her room to make a phone call. They were fine with that. Almost five minutes later, she came back. Her momma desperately wanted to make them a nice dinner as a peace offering, where they could sit down and talk about Malinda's wish to go to art school.

Malinda went to her room to make the phone call to Sam; but before she did, she looked at herself in the mirror. She saw within one day she had changed her life. She did not feel desperate. She felt relieved. She looked into the mirror again. She did not see a coward, but a person who wanted to grow, to live.

Symbolically, she got into the shower to wash off the rest of her old thoughts. She put on a colorful dress with a beautiful bow in her hair which implied that she had wrapped everything up her with parents.

As she dialed Sam's number, she contemplated what she would say. When he answered, she said, "Thank you. I have spoken the truth to my parents, and it worked. I am going to have dinner with them tonight. I have learned that open honest communication solves a lot of problems."

"I'm happy for you Malinda. When you are ready to go to the art store, please let me know."

She spent the weekend becoming ever closer to her parents. They agreed to support her to go to the two-year art school program, starting that very summer. When she called Sam to tell him how her weekend went, he had a similar weekend with his family. By coincidence, since Sam liked art too, he also decided to attend the Art school in the summer.

They went to the art store to buy supplies for the

project they would work on together. Malinda paid her debt to Sam when she bought him a double dipped chocolate banana split sundae with an assortment of colorful sprinkles, a few cherries, sprinkled with walnuts on top.

When the server sat the sundae before Sam, she placed a large paper napkin on the table. She asked if Malinda would like to have an extra spoon. Sam replied, "Of course not!" She can have her own. Please bring another one. I will pay for it." Malinda spoke up, "No, I will have a small spoon."

When the server returned with a small spoon, Sam allowed Malinda to have the first bite. Before he knew it, Malinda had slid the sundae before her and was generously enjoying the sundae. Seeing her so happy, Sam ordered another sundae for himself. She grinned at Sam. "I forgot to tell you that I really like chocolate." That was one of the best afternoons she had in a long time.

When Sam's sundae came out, Malinda was

finishing up. He put his hand over his sundae and ate it like he thought she would lean over to devour it. It was a beautiful day for both of them.

After Sam got home, Jasmine was sitting at the kitchen table. She asked, "Sam did you choose that girl over me?"

"No Jasmine. Are you talking about Malinda?

"You know I'm talking about her."

"She had a little problem. I wanted to help her completely like I would help you if you had a problem, Jasmine."

"You met her a short while ago. What kind of problem would you be able to help her with?"

"Jasmine, she almost asked the same question you asked. She thought I could not help her, but I was able to help her."

"What was wrong with her?"

"Coach Van Damme would not tell her where Tommy was. I told her he had moved to Europe. She started bawling. I asked her why. She said that

Tommy was supposed to marry her."

"Oh no Sam. That girl is crazy. I saw how she was questioning Tommy. I actually talked to her."

"Well after I told her the answer, she confessed that her parents were pressuring her to marry Tommy. I helped her by recommending that she tell her parents the truth. You know, they responded favorably to her. I helped her so she had to buy me a sundae."

"Her parents were pressuring her?"

"Yes, she stood up for herself. I was really happy for her. I encouraged her to pursue art. She is going to enroll in the two-year art program. She seems relaxed and a lot of fun to be around."

"Sam that was nice of you. Be careful. She might hold you to something."

"Like what?"

"Like dating. Maybe marriage."

"Well, that is not a bad thing for me. You know how much I like painting. I am going to enroll in the art school too. So not only did I help Malinda and her parents, but I also helped myself decide what I should do after high school. We went to the art store. Within a few days, she was happier. Her parents were proud of her for expressing her feelings to them, absolutely telling them the simple truth."

"You may be right that your influence had a positive effect on all four of you. Are you going to tell momma that you have decided to go to art school?"

"Sure I am."

"Tell me what?" Cashmere asked.

"Momma you know how much I like painting. I have decided to go to art school. Jasmine can tell you later how I came to that decision."

"Actually, that doesn't matter that much to me. I heard most of it. Merely to decide, has made me feel good. You are going to do well."

Jasmine said, "I cain't wait to tell Marylou that Tommy left the country for nothing."

Jasmine headed down to Marylou's house to speak to her face to face. Missy answered the door and sent Jasmine straight to Marylou's bedroom.

Chapter 12

Jasmine knocked on the door. "Marylou." She opened the door to let Jasmine in. She noticed that Marylou was not her usual self, so she hesitated to reveal the reason for her visit. She asked, "How was your day, Marylou?"

"It was good Jasmine. And yours?"

"It was good. Why are you so laid-back Marylou?"

"It feels like I have brain fog. Cain't think. Cain't sleep. I got a little stressed because River is thinking about changing his major from journalism to music and dance. He called me on the telephone this evening. He told me that it was like my momma gave him so much confidence that he thinks that music and dance is his calling."

"Marylou, what if it is? Would you want to hold him back?"

"Not at all. But I do not really like dance and music. My entire focus has been on becoming a journalist. We may not have that much in common now."

"Well, since he transferred schools, will he still be going to Monroe County High?"

"Yes, but it's not the same as taking an advanced class together."

Jasmine nudged her. "It will work out Marylou. I don't mean to be insensitive; but I gotta tell you about Tommy."

"What about Tommy?"

"Tommy left the country for nothing. The girl that Tommy was supposed to marry is now going out with Sam. They really hit it off."

"Don't tell me anymore! What is this world coming to?"

Jasmine said, "It may be a better match between

Sam and Malinda."

"Who is Malinda?" Marylou asked.

Jasmine answered, "That is the girl's name. She has encouraged Sam to study art in the two-year program."

Marylou said, "You all should be happy for Sam."

Jasmine said, "Yes, I am. He talks like he has a purpose in life now."

"There are so many things changing. I'm trying to keep up Jasmine."

"Don't sweat the small things, Marylou. You know my daddy showed up at my basketball practice today."

"You have got to be kidding me."

"No, I'm not kidding. In this small town, things get around quickly. Someone must have told him that momma was volunteering. Momma is looking better and better every day. Momma said they always come back. Daddy used to say that momma should be thankful about her marriage to him because a lot of women would like to be in her shoes. I never liked him telling her that."

"How did she handle your dad showing up?"

"Thank God, she wasn't there. You know we will be starting the basketball season in a couple of weeks. Momma knows how to handle it."

"Okay keep me posted. Before you leave, my aunt told me she could get me on at the Mobile Press this summer. She said if I wanted to, I could stay with her."

"That's exciting Marylou. Have you decided?"

"Almost. I talked with River. Right after he told me what he was going to do, I told him what I was thinking about doing. He sounded torn."

"Perhaps, he can work there too."

"Who would he stay with? Not my aunt. Anyway, I got to finish my homework. We can talk later."

Coach Van Damme called a special meeting with the volunteers on Thursday. Wouldn't you know it, Cashmere's ex-husband showed up. No other volunteers showed up. Coach Van Damme asked the team to run a mile and come back. While they were running, he met with Jasmine's parents.

Coach Van Damme said, "The basketball team really appreciates your volunteer spirit. We have filled several slots for our volunteers. We only have one slot left for a volunteer. That person will have a dual role. The volunteer would have to practice drills with the team on Thursdays and be available to chaperone on Fridays.

"Mr. Summers. Ms. Summers. After watching the team's response, I have decided that we would like to offer you the final spot Ms. Summers. Thanks again for your support. Mr. Summers, you can do a good service by regularly attending the games. Perhaps, you could volunteer again next year. We will see you in a couple of weeks at the first game in Excel. Also, thank you for your support."

In other words, Coach Van Damme kept Mr. Summers away from Ms. Summers and there was not anything Ms. Summers had to do. When Jasmine heard what happened, she told Marylou, "I knew momma would handle the potential conflict with my daddy if he had served as a volunteer. I was wrong. It was Coach Van Damme that handled it."

The girls played their first basketball game at Excel. It was amazing. Jasmine scored eighteen of the forty-six points. They played the next game in Atmore. It was a repeat of the first win. Next on the roster was Uriah then Beatrice. There were several players that were dominant, but not with the intensity of Jasmine. In a spectacular way, she could not miss. The girls kept the momentum during the entire season because there were no injuries. They finished first. It was an amazing season.

Jasmine's dad attended every one of her games. It made her very happy. Her mom was not as impressed. He brought the woman that she saw when she was leaving work several months ago. By the way she was a tall natural blonde with wavy hair. Of course, she was a white woman, five feet nine inches, with a voluptuous shape as an accessory to her white skin, which made Cashmere question, "Why do Black men always do that?"

Cashmere never missed one of the away games. Neither did she miss one single practice. Her consistency in overseeing the drills, as well as taking part in the drills, brought her a number of compliments. She looked pretty darn good. She was in as good a shape as Jasmine was.

Coach Van Damme was thrilled with the team's success and applauded Ms. Summers for her dedication to the team. He received an award for teacher of the year.

Going toward summer, the girls had to decide how they wanted to spend their summer. Marylou decided to go to Mobile for the summer to work part-time at the Mobile press. Jasmine decided to return to the basketball camp in Sarasota-Bradenton. Malinda enrolled in the art school program. Cashmere scheduled her first date.

Chapter 13

All of the girls had a plan that worked out good for the summer except Cashmere. She was going absolutely crazy. You may question why she was going crazy when the basketball season had gone well. She had gotten in tip top shape. But it was this little thing that God gave us that pricks our heart when something is totally not right. It is called the conscience. You see, Cashmere felt like a hypocrite.

She had slammed her ex-husband because in her mind, he was obviously dating a white woman. She had said, "We don't do that in Alabama." In fact, if she went on her scheduled date with Coach Van Damme, she would be going out with a white man.

Now how was she any different than her husband? And if there were isolated cases where it did happen in Alabama, and it worked out well, she had not seen it. She believed that she should not rock the boat.

Cashmere worked with a young woman who told her a story that was so disturbing that she could not get it out of her head. The young woman's brother met Cashmere along with her co-worker in the parking lot of a shopping center to give her co-worker a document that their momma sent. After her brother left, Cashmere commented, "Your brother looks so different from you."

The co-worker asked, "What do you mean?"

Cashmere tried to explain without being offensive. "Well, in a lot of ways you two look different. You have a slim build, and you have a medium height. He has a stocky build and much shorter than you. He looks so much older than you. And his skin is really different."

The young co-worker went on to explain to

Cashmere. "My momma had my brother when she was fifteen years old. She had me when she was almost forty-two years old.

"My brother's daddy is from Africa. My daddy is White. Actually, I am part Jewish. My momma did not have any other children after my brother was born. She never married. Finally, she thought she had found love. She believed that the man she worked for loved her too. At that point, she had a relationship with him. Since the man was prominent, he suddenly fell out of love with her when he found out she was pregnant. So, she had to leave town, alone and pregnant."

After remembering that example, equally important to Cashmere, was not wanting to be a hypocrite. Cashmere cancelled her date and never rescheduled. She was so ashamed that she closed dating for the entire summer. Jasmine and Marylou's junior year was the same as their sophomore year except for the fact that Cashmere decided not to be a volunteer for the basketball team Jasmine's junior year. As a matter of fact, Cashmere did not support the basketball team Jasmine's senior year either. You would never believe who became the new volunteer. Do you give up? You might as well give up. Here is a hint for you. She went to a talent show. Next, she showed out. Yes, you guessed it. Missy Marshall.

Remember when Marylou and Missy Marshall went to the talent show where River performed like a person making a slam dunk at a basketball game? Powerful performance! Missy Marshall's support was undeniably exhilarating at the talent show! So now she had a platform to use her rah-rah spirit almost every day of the week. Now that Cashmere did not have that commitment, she decided to learn everything she could about opening her own business. By the end of Jasmine's senior year in high school, she opened Cashmere's Spa, the very first one in town.

Cashmere's Spa had a nail station, a massage room, a skincare room, and a hair salon with one barber and two stylists. No one knew that Cashmere had that type of capability to open her own business. It was amazing how motivated people were in the community. Because she had dreamed about opening her own business, she had been gathering data as to what would do well in Monroeville. Her preliminary finding involved chatting with the women in the city. She learned that many women had to travel out of town up to an hour or more to get services like facials and massages. And precisely at the right time, she found a building that would be perfect for starting her first business. She rented an old vacant five-bedroom house with plenty of parking and a lot of yard space. With a little paint and some creativity, she would turn that old house into a home away from home with her lineup of pampering services.

She advertised on several social media websites. Especially since Malinda and Sam had finished the art school program, they were available to help out with the cosmetic touchups to the building during the summer. Jasmine received a basketball scholarship to the University of Alabama and decided to go to summer school at Alabama after she graduated from high school. She had a little time to help her momma out before she left for summer school. Excitement was all around their family.

The layout of the spa was at best simply country elegant. The foyer in the house became the reception area. When you walked into the spa, the air smelled like lavender. Sam refinished an old maple desk for the receptionist area. In that area was where customers checked in, and the receptionist served in dainty glasses, fresh lemonade, water infused with cucumber and mint leaves daily.

Sam and Jasmine spray painted the outside of the entire house powder blue, spray painted the window frames and shutters white. Malinda, Jasmine, and Sam painted the inside of the house a soft sage green with cream trim. The massage room had a small electric waterfall that was about six feet tall, which sounded solely like a person had opened the window to hear the ocean. Sam painted a beautiful sunset over the ocean on one of the walls in the room. In the skincare room, Cashmere bought a large painting of women of all nationalities and skin colors to place on the wall. She had a steamer and other basic tools for skincare. This was the smallest room. The bathroom had a shower that worked well for clients that received a variety of skincare body treatments. She stocked the bathroom showers with lavender towels.

The open area had a huge television with different ocean scenes around the world. There was relaxing soulful music as the backdrop. Cashmere had an extended piano version of Barry White's song *I've Got So Much to Give.* That song was her favorite on the playlist. The stylists' station was simply elegant with small panels that separated each stylist.

The nail area included four chairs. Each chair offered a massage. Near the nail area, the spa offered a retail center which included nail polish, skincare products, shampoos, conditioners and gift certificates for purchase.

Even when people did not have various services scheduled, they would come to buy their products, sit in the front yard with a glass of lemonade under the two largest magnolia trees that practically covered the front yard. And if that were not inviting enough, patrons could sit on the front porch in the rocking chair with a cool glass of the cucumber water. On Fridays, Cashmere baked homemade brownies served with ice cream made with an old ice cream machine that churned her homemade recipe into a smooth vanilla ice cream. The smell of the fresh baked brownies hurried people in that were only taking a casual walk in the community.

Immediately, her business increased when the word got out about the homemade brownies and ice cream. Following that boom in business, she offered brownies and ice cream on Saturday too. In the backyard there was a swing set, monkey bar, a slide, and a sandbox for the children.

Jasmine asked her momma to put a basketball goal up for the children. As you can tell, her momma knew that Jasmine had been wanting a basketball hoop for herself, so she had it placed in the backyard at the spa. Adults always supervised the children while playing. Since it was not that much to do in the community, the parents would bring the babysitter along with the child and the grandmomma sometimes. It was genuinely a country affair. It was a home environment away from home that attracted most everybody.

After Cashmere got her stylists, nail techs, massage therapists and estheticians hired, she had an open house. The sign read *Cashmere's Spa* with the byline *We're Here for You.* There was a big write-up in the newspaper that was quite impressive. The article read, "She made her customers feel like they were at home." Cashmere's Spa had no competition.

Now, it was Jasmine's turn. Jasmine arrived at

Alabama excited about her new life. Cashmere and Sam were so happy for her. Even Malinda came along to Alabama with the family.

Jasmine would not have a roommate until the fall. Her family helped her move all of her personal things into her room. They visited with her about five or six hours. After that, they headed back to Monroeville. Jasmine had reached the first part of her goal toward making professional basketball. While meditating on her accomplishment, she decided to take a hike around the campus.

You may well understand that she would go directly to the basketball court. Once there, she imagined dribbling down the court, going into the corner to make her consistent three point shot before the buzzer went off. Jasmine looked into the bleachers and imagined the crowd going wild. She saw her dad. She saw her momma. She saw Marylou. She saw Sam. She saw Malinda. She saw Coach Van Damme. She saw Tommy. And then she saw Skyler.

But for some reason, he seemed real.

She looked away and looked back and it was for real. It appeared to be Skyler. In a flash she thought, "Skyler was coming to play basketball. Is that him?"

Then someone yelled. "Hey Jasmine!" It was Skyler. She passed out. All of the excitement had taken a toll on her. He ran to her and asked, "Jasmine, are you okay? Jasmine!"

Jasmine looked at him, "Skyler, is that you?"

Skyler said, "Yes Jasmine. I heard that you were coming for the summer, so I decided to come. I knew you would come to the basketball court. So, I have been waiting for you. What took you so long to recognize me?"

Jasmine responded, "I…I don't know. I was so into the moment that I had made it here to play basketball. I was dreaming about the game. Everything seemed so real."

Skyler congratulated her. "What a big achievement. Have you talked to your coach yet?"

"No. I have not Skyler."

Skyler said, "I can take you to him."

"I thought the coach was a woman."

"She has been replaced Jasmine."

"No one told me that."

"Jasmine it was quick."

"Replaced by who?"

"By my dad, Coach Luke Chadsworth."

"Your dad?"

"Who is your coach Skyler?"

"My dad."

"So, he is coaching both women and men?"

"Only until they find the replacement. They are almost about to decide on the replacement. Do not worry. Dad will be good for you. Have you eaten? Let's go get something to eat."

"Okay. That will be good. I have not eaten anything."

Skyler asked, "What would you like to eat?"

"A turkey burger would be great."

"Not sure where we can get a turkey burger, but I can take you somewhere to get a beef burger."

So off they went. They had a lot to catch up on. They talked for about an hour. Jasmine learned that Skyler would be living on campus and when he told her that he was interested in a young freshman that he had met, she took a deep breath then slowly blew it out. Without a word, she reasoned that it was for the best if she were going to make pro basketball. She remained focused even in that instance.

Jasmine went on to tell Skyler about her momma's new spa. Additionally, she told him that Sam really liked Malinda and that she would not be surprised if they got married in a year or two. Skyler suggested that they stop by his daddy's office for a quick visit.

When they arrived at Coach Chadsworth's office, he was on a phone call. That being the case, they patiently waited for him. By now, Jasmine could hardly keep her eyes open. For that reason, she wanted to go to her room and get some rest. About five minutes later, he ended the call. He asked Skyler, "Who is this young woman that you have here?"

Skyler answered, "This is the young freshman I met."

Jasmine looked puzzled. "You told me you had met a freshman."

Skyler smiled, "Yes, I told you that. You are the freshman! Who did you think I was talking about?"

Jasmine was embarrassed. "I thought you were talking about someone you met last year."

"Oh no Jasmine. I was talking about you. As I said, I have been waiting for you." Jasmine was speechless.

Coach Chadsworth jumped in really quickly. "Jasmine, my son said you have an unbelievable three-point shot. Is that true?" Although tired, it was no time for Jasmine to be shy.

She came alive. "Yes Coach, I have been told that I do."

"Well, I'm going to put a schedule together for you.

We can start your program right away. Would that be ok?"

"Why yes Coach! I didn't know we would do that so soon."

"Why wait? You do not know anyone other than my son. So, you would have time to get a jump start on the season."

"Yes, Coach Chadsworth. Thank you. Sounds terrific."

Jasmine only registered for two classes. She could easily use her time to practice her game. She was thrilled. It was a fabulous day.

Chapter 14

As soon as Coach Chadsworth completed Jasmine's training schedule, she started training the very next day with Skyler. For the most part, her schedule included weight training two days per week, as well as, running three days per week. On her weight training days, she also completed several basketball drills. Besides that, she trained with others on the men's basketball team who had registered for summer classes. They looked like giants over her or as they say in the South, 'beef fed kids.' Nevertheless, Jasmine did not let their size intimidate her.

Jasmine's training was exactly what she wanted and obviously what she needed. Her demeanor was serious, primarily focused. She was closer to her goal of making the pros. By the end of the summer, Jasmine had put on ten pounds of pure, solid muscles. With about two weeks before fall classes would start, Cashmere asked Jasmine to come home for the weekend. She needed a break as much as Jasmine did. Coach Chadsworth felt that Jasmine deserved it; therefore, he was happy that she would get a chance to go home before classes started again.

Especially, over the summer, Cashmere's Spa had grown a lot. She had to hire more people to cover the added hours. The new Spa hours changed from 10 a.m. to nine a.m. and from six p.m. to seven p.m. To begin with, her business was unbelievable. Actually, Sam and Malinda helped her get the upstairs ready for customers who purchased a *One Day Spa Escape*. She named the upstairs room 'The Relaxation Zone.' In this room, there were four lounges. Each lounge had a fluffy robe lying across it.

In between each lounge was a selection of books

and magazines. Cashmere had to buy several copies of the book, *She Couldn't Spell Debt,* because it looked like some of the customers wanted to borrow the book as soon as she replaced it. And when asked to return it, one customer said, "I'm so sorry. I have not finished reading it yet. I promise I will bring it back as soon as I finish. I could not find it because my daughter was reading it. I hope that'll be all right." Cashmere came up with a new promotion, buy a *One Day Spa Escape* and receive a gift, the book "*She Couldn't Spell Debt.*"

There were three counters in the lounge room. One had an assortment of herbal teas, gourmet coffee and water infused with cucumbers or lime slices or strawberries. Another counter had fruit displays. The third counter had apple spiced muffins lined up with different finger sandwiches. Anyone who bought the *One Day Spa Escape* could sit in the room as long as they wanted before their spa service, between their spa service, or at the end of their spa service with available snacks all day long. They could come as soon as the doors opened and stay until they closed. Only four packages were available for purchase each day.

When Jasmine made it to Monroeville, she called her momma to let her know that she was in town and headed to visit her daddy. Once Jasmine knocked on the door, it took her daddy about three or four minutes to open the door. After he finally opened the door, she said, "Daddy were you sleeping?"

"No. I was trying to put on some clothes before I answered the door. When did you get here?"

"A few minutes ago, daddy. I called momma to let her know that I was coming to see you first." Boy, he was happy because he did not get the opportunity to go to Alabama with her; but, for her to make him her first stop, erased the pain.

"Honey, how are you doing? You look great."

"Thanks daddy. I am happy. I have been working out very hard."

She went into details about everything she had experienced at Alabama and felt that was the place for her. After spending the entire afternoon with Jasmine, her daddy got another surprise. Cashmere invited him over to have dinner with the family. He could not believe it. On top of that, he was curious about how she would treat him. When he arrived at Cashmere's house with Jasmine, Sam and Malinda were already there.

Cashmere grabbed her daughter and gave her a monstrous bear hug. She even gave her ex-husband a light hug with a tender kiss on his cheek. That scared Geronimo! Caught him totally off guard. Once again, completely surprised, he looked off, wondering what she was thinking about. Was this the same woman he was married to a few years ago? He went along with it, hoping that she would not lower the boom on him.

The night before, Cashmere carefully prepared the dinner. She made a cucumber salad for an appetizer, which consisted of cucumbers, grape tomatoes, red onions with a red wine vinaigrette dressing. She roasted a fifteen-pound turkey. She sautéed cabbage with garlic and onions, green beans and she made cilantro rice with a zest of lime. And lastly, you could say she was saving her daily allowance of carbs to finish the meal with a sweet potato soufflé with a glazed pecan topping, that would make you holler. She also prepared a peach flavored iced tea in addition to having a bottle of chilled Pinot Grigio for the adults.

Geronimo took one bite of the roasted turkey. A feeling of comfort, particularly familiarity, went straight to his heart, and he started to meditate silently. Not one woman, friend, or girlfriend was able to cook like this. He started to reminisce. Going down memory lane in prayer he said, "I needed to be home. Lord the seasoning was good. The temperature was perfect. The atmosphere was pleasant. I felt like someone loved me. What am I going to do?" That was his silent prayer.

It was such a beautiful dinner. Everyone sort of caught up on each other's news. Jasmine told everyone that she was the only female basketball player at the school for the summer. Then, Skyler's daddy gave her a training schedule which allowed her to practice with the men's basketball team. Cashmere asked her, "Did they go easy on you, or did they play with you like you were a man?"

"Momma, they played with me like I was a grown man who was their enemy. That was excellent training for me. One guy charged me. As he tried to take the ball away from me, I did a crossover with my right hand, went around the back with my left hand, dribbled between my legs and he fell down. I did not show him one ounce of compassion. I dunked on him. The players and the coach called timeout. Momma, the next guy dropped back on me, daring me to shoot. I dropped back behind the three-point line and swished it. Coach chewed him out. He asked him, "What are you doing? Don't you know she is dangerous?""'

Looking worried, Cashmere said, "I hope they don't get upset with you."

"Ah momma. Basketball is all about moves and skills. You know that because you played the game before, and you played with me. Remember? That is really going to help me make pro. I totally enjoyed it. They got a chance to see too that I had potential. I hope that they got that on tape. Oh, and I got a chance to play with Skyler too. So, I will be so much more ahead when the season starts because I would have had a lot of competitive tutors to help me improve my game."

Jasmine's dad commented, "Honey, I cain't wait to see your first game. You certainly got those moves from your momma. Will you let me know your schedule as soon as possible so I can organize my work?"

"Yes daddy. Of course, I will. I got a few moves

from you too, I am sure. I just did not get a chance to play you in a game of one on one. But it's okay."

Sam teased her a little bit. "You look like a professional athlete already. Looks like you grew a little bit, and you are showing off your pumped-up muscles. Did vitamins make you look like that?"

Jasmine loved every minute of it. "I'm eating well, working out hard and sleeping hard. I am so happy that my classes are not very difficult. Got that? What is happening with you, big brother?"

"Well Malinda and I are working Wednesday afternoons at the spa painting and drawing portraits of customers. It has been really good for us. We have both applied for positions at an Advertising Company in Birmingham. Malinda can tell you what else she has been doing."

Malinda excitedly replied, "One of the parents in the spa asked me to help her child because she believed that she had a talent for art. And it is true. The young child does have a strong talent for art, so

I am tutoring her. That is going well. My parents are really happy for me. After I attended art school, they learned more about me in reference to my talents and goals that they had not noticed. They are really proud of me."

Jasmine complimented her. "Malinda that is great! I really think you have been a wonderful inspiration for our Sam. I don't think I ever told you that."

Malinda's eyes filled with tears as Jasmine spoke. "You have it backwards. He encouraged me to speak to my parents and stand up for myself. I was living a life that was stressful. Sam gave me the courage to express my feelings to my parents. He has been with me every step of the way. He has changed my life."

Sam smiled. "I'm happy to hear you say that Malinda. There was something about you from the beginning that appealed to me. That is why I would like to spend the rest of my life with you, if you would have me." Then Sam got down on one knee, pulled a ring out of his pocket and asked, "Malinda, will you marry me?"

She asked, "Are you sure?"

"Yes, I have been sure for over a year. I was waiting to see if, you were sure."

"I'm sure. Yes. I will marry you."

Cashmere looked at Jasmine. Jasmine looked at her daddy. Then they all looked at each other before anyone got up. Then Sam's daddy, got up, walked over to them. He reached out to hug each of them while saying, "Congratulations son. Congratulations Malinda. We named my son after my father. My father named me Geronimo after his favorite hero in the United States. I pray that you two never make the mistake that I made." A tear dropped from his eye. After that, he thanked Cashmere for inviting him over. He could only say that everything was great, and it was time to leave.

Cashmere had never seen the tender side of Geronimo in that way in a long time. She wanted him to stay. As he was walking towards the door, the doorbell rang. Geronimo looked back surprised that the doorbell rang.

"Cashmere whispered, "I wonder who that is. Jasmine, get the door."

When she opened the door, it was Coach Van Damme with a bouquet of colorful flowers. "Coach Van Damme what are you doing here?"

"Hey Jasmine. What are you doing here? I came to pay a visit to Cashmere."

Geronimo said, "Hi Coach. Good to see you. I was on my way out. Enjoy your visit."

Cashmere pleaded, "Geronimo, why don't you stay, in order to chat with Coach Van Damme." She did not want him to leave feeling downtrodden, after such a nice dinner and the recent engagement of Sam and Malinda.

"Thanks Cashmere. I appreciate the offer, but I should get on home because I have a few things I need to do."

Coach Van Damme smirked. "Ok. Sorry you

have to go. See you around." Then Coach walked over to Cashmere, slyly touched her hand while giving her a colorful bunch of flowers that he had gotten from the flower shop where she once worked. Then he reached over to hug her while mouthing, "I have missed you. How are you doing? You look amazing."

After Geronimo saw that, he walked out the door without saying another word. Before he left the front porch, his heart began fluttering out of control. He felt so weak that his knees buckled. He felt like he would pass out. That interaction he witnessed between Cashmere and Coach Van Damme almost forced the life out of him, like when a vacuum cleaner forcefully picks up dirt.

He said to himself, "Here, I'm leaving my house where I lived with my family. Another man has come into my house to take my woman. And there is nothing that I can do about it because I am the one who walked away. What have I done? He is in there with my children and my future daughter-in-law.

That is plain demoralizing. I could simply die."

By the time Geronimo had reached his car, the one tear that he had shed inside the house had become a flood of tears by the time he had gotten into his car. It looked as if a water hose sprayed him. He put the key in the ignition, decided that he should go back and see what Coach Van Damme was doing to his wife; however, as he tried to get out of the car, his knees buckled because he was paralyzed by the fear of what he would see.

Jasmine, Sam, and Malinda looked puzzled how Coach Van Damme had come in and treated Cashmere. She accepted the hug, the gorgeous flowers while responding, "Thank you. I am doing well. Been a little busy with my business. How are you?"

"I'm doing better, now that I have seen you."

Jasmine thought "What in the world is he doing? Why is he acting like that? Why is momma looking like a deer in the headlights of a car, vulnerable and timid?" Jasmine decided that she had better intervene because her mother looked so uncomfortable. She had not dated anyone else other than Geronimo; hence, she did not know what to do.

To the contrary, Jasmine made it worse when she said, "Coach Van Damme would you like something to eat. Momma cooked a fabulous meal."

"Well, if that is not too much trouble. I have not eaten anything. I can take it to go since you were not expecting my visit."

Jasmine insisted, "No sir Coach Van Damme. Sit right down. I will fix you a plate. Momma, why don't you have a seat too."

Jasmine thought that eating the food would take the attention off of Cashmere, instead it made him more focused on her. Cashmere was looking for a way out; but it was too late. Sam pulled the chair out for his momma. All five of them sat down at the table.

Coach made a pitiful statement. "It's been a while

since I have eaten any home cooked meal. Extremely kind of you all."

Sam chimed in, "No problem at all Coach Van Damme. Momma cooks meals like this all the time for us."

After Coach began eating the food, he started moaning. "Oh my, this is simply delicious. Cashmere, I did not know you could cook like this." He reached out to touch her hand. Once his hand connected to her hand, he said, "You are like the capable wife. You can pretty much do everything. You are a business owner. You cook. You take good care of yourself. Look at you. Wonderful. You take care of your children. You help others. I am just fascinated by you." By now, Coach could not control himself. He was talking as if no one else was in the room.

He continued, "Furthermore, you are five ten, about one hundred sixty-five pounds of pure curves. Your hair smells divine. It is so silky. Your skin is buttery. Your walk is mesmerizing."

Then he took her down memory lane.

"Remember when I encouraged you to volunteer to assist the basketball team after I saw you and Jasmine play? I only told you it would be good for the girls. Now, I can tell you it was beneficial for me too when you volunteered. You made every single practice. You attended every single away game. I anticipated seeing you every practice, every game. And then, suddenly you could not support the team anymore. I was disappointed, dejected that you left. So, I had to tell you how I felt. That is one of the reasons why I wanted to bring you flowers."

He picked up momentum while still holding her hand. "I have never forgotten your sacrifice. Maybe you can come by the gymnasium from time to time."

Cashmere pulled her hand back from his hand, pushed her chair back from the table, stood up and broke away.

She asked, "Would you like me to get you

something else?"

"No, everything is perfect."

"Cashmere interjected, "Tomorrow I have to get up early for our spiritual service. I have to get my clothes ready."

Then Malinda blurted out, "Coach Van Damme, we got engaged a short while ago."

"Malinda, I thought you were going to marry Tom."

Sam asked, "Who is Tom?"

Malinda explained, "He is talking about his nephew Tommy. Remember he was the one who asked me to marry him when I turned eighteen. You helped me get over it.

Sam said, "Oh yeah. I remember."

Malinda did not skip a beat. "Well Coach Van Damme, where did you find that list of qualities of a capable wife?"

"I believe it's in Proverbs chapter thirty-one of the holy scriptures. Almost an entire chapter is dedicated to how to be a capable wife."

"Ms. Summers, do you have a Bible? I am curious. I want to look at that now."

"Right now?"

"Yes, if you don't mind Ms. Summers."

"Sam, will you get it for her?"

"Where is it?"

"It's in the first drawer in the buffet next to the silverware."

"Ok. Got it. Here it is Malinda."

As Malinda turned to the table of contents, she saw the book of Proverbs. She turned to chapter thirty-one.

Sam asked Malinda, "Do you think that we can read it together a little later?"

"I suppose so. I got a little carried away. I can get my parents' copy. We can read it tomorrow on our break at the spa. I better get on home now. Sam, can you drop me off?"

"Yes, I can drop off my newly engaged girlfriend."

Malinda expressed tenderness when she said, "Good evening everyone. I will see you at the spiritual service tomorrow." Jasmine took the opportunity to leave also.

"Well momma, I'm going to run down to Marylou's house. I'll be back in about an hour."

Cashmere said, "No Jasmine. I want you to go with your brother to chaperone them because he might not make it back. Then you two can stop by to see Marylou on your way back. Remember that we have to get up early in the morning to eat breakfast before we leave."

Coach Van Damme did not appear that he was ready to leave, so Cashmere helped him nicely. "Coach I guess it's time to end the night. Thank you so very much for the flowers. I want to walk Sam and Malinda out. We can all walk out together."

"Oh yes. You are welcome Ms. Summers. I can walk out with you all. I can come back another time to finish our conversation."

Cashmere stuck out her hand to shake Coach Van Damme's hand. He shook her hand bringing her closer to him. But she moved away like she was playing dodge ball. He thought it was cute. Certainly, he did not force it. He walked down the sidewalk to his car and drove off.

Everyone had left. Cashmere was all alone with her thoughts. She started reminiscing about the evening. Everyone looked so happy. Her meal was tasty. She considered how a little over two to three years ago, she was in the same position as Geronimo when she ran into him with another woman. She recalled how she tried to keep her dignity without breaking down emotionally.

As soon as she got into the car, she released an avalanche of tears. The song playing on the radio when she was leaving the scene brought on her tears. It was Whitney Houston singing *Where Do Broken Hearts Go*? Right after that song played on the radio, Al Greene's song came on, *Let's Stay Together.* She wondered if that in fact happened to Geronimo when he got into his car earlier in the evening. If so, she could seriously empathize with him; except, would he feel jealous that Coach Van Damme brought her flowers?

Cashmere was undoubtedly jealous when she saw Geronimo with another woman for the first time since their divorce. Although Cashmere noticed that he had changed somewhat, why was she so concerned about his feelings? Well, she reasoned that he was the father of their two beautiful children. Once upon a time the entire family lived in the house. Cashmere knew that Geronimo may have assumed that he would find out if she brought another man to their house. He also knew that Jasmine and Sam loved him so much that out of respect for their children, she would not have done that. As often as Cashmere had attended spiritual services, she had never heard of the 'capable wife.' She wondered if that was what she was missing in her marriage to Geronimo. She was glad that Malinda did not take her Bible because she would read Proverbs, chapter thirty-one as soon as she finished cleaning up the kitchen and preparing her clothes for their spiritual service.

Moreover, she questioned that if the Bible gave the qualifications for a capable wife, were there qualifications for a capable husband? Her head was spinning. Cashmere was sure she would eventually find it; but then again, she was much more concerned how to find out what applied to her.

She finished her chores and was ready to read the entire passage when Jasmine walked in. She read it with Jasmine, and both were surprised. Although it was not in modern terms, both could see how the principles applied still. They did not question how they could receive help from studying it. By the time they finished, Sam walked in. Cashmere said, "Sam I would love to talk with you after you two read Proverbs chapter thirty-one. Your sister and I learned a lot."

"Ok momma. I will."

They went to their rooms. Cashmere was so intrigued with what she read. She compared what she read to what she did while she was married to Geronimo. Unknowingly, she was doing many of those things mentioned.

She googled marriage and she found a website that had several interesting articles on the importance of good communication in marriage and how to solve problems. Bing! Bing! Bing! That was what she and Geronimo had gone through. She reasoned that they loved each other; yet their communication and problem-solving skills were awful.

In one article, she learned that when women have problems, they want to talk about their feelings to their husbands while they listen. The husband wants to solve the problems that the wife talks about without realizing that most of the time, as the wife talks it out, she can solve the problem herself. So that interaction, more often than not, produced conflict.

The article also said that when a husband does not listen to his wife without interrupting her to provide a solution as to what she should do, it makes her feel depressed or belittled. The husband has to let his wife, who is his partner, know that he fully understands and empathizes with her dilemma before he suggests a solution. Oftentimes, the wife only wants the husband to be a good listener. Cashmere felt relieved that she had found that website.

Everyone got up early the next morning. Jasmine and Sam had finished preparing breakfast for the family. They were so excited that they got a chance to spend time with their daddy. Now they were off to their spiritual service.

Chapter 15

After their spiritual service, Cashmere and the kids went home to finish up leftovers from Saturday's dinner. Jasmine picked up the conversation in the car.

"Momma are you interested in Coach Van Damme?"

"No. Jasmine, I do not have time for Coach Van Damme. I have my children that I'm interested in, my health, my business and now the wedding if Sam and Malinda need help."

Jasmine continued, "Oh Yeah. That is right. Sam, what did Malinda's parents say about your engagement?"

"They were thrilled. They really want us to be

happy. Malinda and I did talk about when would be a good time to get married. What do you think momma?"

"I think that you two should make the decision. I would say if it were me, probably in the late spring in case you get a job out of town."

Sam agreed. "Yes. That is what we thought. On the other hand, there is so much planning, which means we would have to prepare months before the wedding and that would throw us in the middle of the basketball season, adding to Jasmine's stress level."

"Jasmine said, "That is true. What about a May wedding? We could plan what I need to get done during spring break."

"Malinda thought April or May would be good. Sounds like a May wedding would be better."

Cashmere asked, "Does Malinda have a lot of pieces in her hope chest?"

"I don't know momma even if she has one."

"Please find out. We can help her with items to put

in there if she does not have one. I can get her a journal so she can keep everything together."

"Oh momma, I'll find out. Also, when I talked to Marylou, she said that Coach Van Damme knew that I was coming in town. Mrs. Marshall told him. He acted as if he were surprised. He used my visit to come see you. He really came to see you." Jasmine giggled.

"Well, my sweet darling Jasmine, I have shut that down. That's the end of it."

The doorbell rang. Jasmine said, "That is probably Coach Van Damme." She ran to the door. "It's daddy."

"Hey daddy, come on in."

"Hey everybody. Hope I did not interrupt anything. Jasmine, I wanted to make sure I saw you before you left. I also wanted to tell Sam that I want to help him with the wedding."

Cashmere said, "Thank you Geronimo. That is what we were talking about a few seconds ago. It will probably be a May wedding. Will that work for you too?

"Sure, it will. That's more than enough time for me to budget my money."

Sam said, "Thank you daddy. I will keep you posted."

"Thanks Sam. Yawl know I could have called, but I wanted to see you all together again. If you do not mind, I would like to talk to your momma for a few minutes alone."

"Sure daddy, we can run down to Marylou's house for at most about a half hour. Is that enough time?"

"It will not take that long; however, that will give me more than enough time." Off they went, closing the door behind them.

Cashmere asked, "Is everything okay Geronimo?"

"Yes. I wanted to share something with you. First of all, thank you again for including me in your dinner arrangements yesterday. When my son asked Malinda to marry him, our engagement flashed before my eyes.

That is why I told him not to make the mistake I did. Not that it is important to you now. Outside of that, I sincerely wanted you to know that I have never loved another woman or been with another woman sexually or done anything inappropriate to another woman while married or after our divorce.

"The woman that you saw me with was a date someone set up. Although I tried going out with her a second time, I acknowledged she was not right for me. I do not know if I will ever marry again because I would compare every woman to you. You were my 'capable wife.' I was specifically too young to know how to handle marriage.

"When Coach Van Damme stopped by yesterday, my heart exploded because I thought he was going to take what once belonged to me. When I saw him kiss you on the cheek, I died inside. When I left, my tears drenched the front of my shirt due to the fact that I could not stop thinking how I messed up, by walking out on my family. Today, my purpose in stopping by is to say to you that I am sorry for how I treated you. Please forgive me. Coach Van Damme seems to be a good person. He beat me fair and square. I hope he treats you and my children better than I treated you all. I kept expecting you to be angry with me when I came over yesterday. But your disposition reassured me of your kindness, of your potential for extending forgiveness to me. That's all I wanted to say."

"Geronimo, thank you. First of all, how do you know about a 'capable wife'?"

"My momma always talked to me about marrying a 'capable wife.' But I did not get the sense of what she was telling me. Now that I am older, I know it involves more than saying I will marry a 'capable wife.' I know that a husband should view his wife as a complement and never feel threatened by her and all the things that she can achieve.

"The relationship between a husband and a wife was the only one in the holy scriptures that said the two must become one flesh. It did not say the same about a parent and a child would become one flesh or any other relationship. The wife was meant to be a complement of her husband. God never refers to a child as being a complement. So, at times, I treated you like a child. Especially, in that manner, I did not honor my marriage mate. Also, please forgive me for my indifference back then. No matter how painful it would be for me to see you with another man, I will do my best to support you as much as I can in whatever way you would like. I will not interfere with your desire to move forward with him."

"Thank you, Geronimo. I am in the frame of mind to understand what you have said. A few years ago, I was still adjusting. I really thank you for pouring your heart out to me. One day, I may be able to do the same. Where I am now is that we should be able to do an excellent job of being involved parents for our children. That is a project we can work on together without remorse."

"I want to leave before the kids come back. Don't

know if my heart can take leaving again with both of them here."

Cashmere walked him to the door. "I needed to hear you say those things. Geronimo, perhaps, my self-esteem will improve."

"You are one of the most strikingly beautiful women I know. I am sorry that I did not make you believe it. I have come to see that actions are louder than words. You see, a man on the street, someone who you did not know, could have told you that you were beautiful, but he could not show you. If he did, that would be improper to do so. I needed to show you that you were beautiful. Even at your lowest point, I could have taken more of an initiative toward you, building you up with actions like putting on some dance music, making you feel wanted and loved by twirling you around in a playful yet romantic way like when we were dating, concluding with an eye-to-eye lock, where I refused to take my eyes off of you. I had a legal right to satisfy you. Since I did not do that,

I failed because I was selfish. I have to live with that the rest of my life.

"Your self-esteem went down after we got married. I noticed it. I take some responsibility for that." He smiled at her, patted her on the back and waved goodbye. His emotions would not allow him to say anything else.

When the youngsters came back, they asked, "Where is daddy?"

"He had to leave. It was the most incredible conversation. He wanted me to feel better about everything that had happened. He really wanted us to do more solid parenting together, supporting each of you in any way that we could. It took a lot for him to tell me those things, to pour his heart out leaving himself vulnerable. Your daddy is really changing."

"Was he upset about Coach Van Damme stopping by?"

"Mind your own business, Jasmine!"

"That is our business momma." Sam blurted out.

"You kids need to get a life." They all laughed.

Sam yelled. "Yeah. Daddy did not like that. I thought Coach was in for a battle. Cause daddy would have won!"

"You guys need to stop it. Jasmine, I want to see how you are going to handle marriage one day. Sam, we will see soon enough how you are going to handle it. So, zip the lip."

Chapter 16

Shortly after Jasmine arrived at the campus, she went down the hallway from her dorm room to register for her classes and ran into River. She asked, "River, what are you doing up here?"

"I got accepted into the journalism program."

"Does Marylou know? No joke, I actually got back from Monroeville a little while ago; yet, she did not say one word."

"She does not know. I wanted to check it out first. You know Marylou was stuck on staying in Mobile. I wasn't that interested in living in Mobile."

"Well, River if you decide to go to school up here, I would be happy to have my cousin with me."

"If you feel that way, I will stay Jasmine. I need a

friend too."

"River, you will not believe this. I have been training with the men's basketball team and it has been the best thing that has happened to me since I arrived. Quite frankly, I have had pure concentration. Not sure if that will continue because my roommate should be checking in today. Gotta finish registration for classes, plus go meet her. Remember Skyler, the guy I met when I went to a basketball camp in Sarasota-Bradenton? He is up here too, playing for the men's basketball team. Yep, you will get a chance to meet him later. I gotta go. I will talk to you later. Send me a text when you are available. You look pretty good cousin River."

"So, do you cousin Jasmine. Muscles everywhere? Okay then."

"Yeah River, I hope you are going to be on the newspaper team for the reason that I will have to have some good articles written about me."

"Okay Jasmine, I must report the facts. Make me

proud of you. Check in with you later cuz."

Skyler ran over to Jasmine as River was leaving. "Hey Jasmine. Glad you are back. How was your trip?"

"Very good Skyler. Very good. My brother got engaged to his girlfriend while we were having dinner with my parents. I expected him to ask his girlfriend to marry him, but not so soon, at least another year."

"Who was the big fellow you were talking to earlier?"

"Wouldn't you like to know? Why do you ask?"

"Sure, I would like to know if I'm going to be your husband."

"Let's talk about that later. I'll introduce you to him."

"Jasmine, where are you running off too?"

"Got a lot to do Skyler. Will send you a text later when I have time to talk."

"So, it's like that? You have been running from me since you were fifteen years old. Why do you keep running from me?"

She yelled back, "You should know why. I'm shy."

Jasmine completed her registration and went back to her room to meet her roommate, Lillie Gray, from South Carolina. She was about six feet tall, very thin, may have been one hundred and fifty pounds with all of her clothes on plus a winter coat. After a brief conversation with Lillie, Jasmine headed to basketball practice, leaving Lillie to find her way to the gym. When Jasmine arrived, the men's basketball team was there, ready to start playing. Jasmine's roommate showed up a few minutes later.

Coach Chadsworth put Skyler and Jasmine on the same team. Lillie was on the opposing team. Coach had Jasmine guard Lillie, both who were coming in as a starter on the women's team. As everyone warmed up, Jasmine talked to Lillie a little bit more. After their warmup, the game started, and the intensity of the game grew.

Lillie was dribbling down court. The little chat

Lillie had with Jasmine was in the past. It appeared that Lillie came to play. As soon as she went up to take the shot, Jasmine jumped up like a kangaroo and blocked the shot. Jasmine said, "Welcome to Alabama." The men were passing the ball to the women to see how they would interact with each other. One of the guys tossed the ball to Jasmine. In the corner of the court, she hit the three-pointer which she consistently made while she was at camp in Sarasota-Bradenton. No doubt about it, by now, she had perfected her signature shot. It was more powerful than before because she had put on ten pounds of unadulterated muscles.

Training with the men for the summer was nothing to laugh at, as Jasmine saw the benefit of her real-deal workouts. When coach Chadsworth switched the team up again, each team ran the ball for the better part of twenty minutes. Then he assigned Skyler to guard Jasmine. They were running toe to toe when Jasmine raised up to hit the three-pointer. Skyler said,

"Show me what you got Jasmine." Jasmine hit the three-pointer and headed back down the court.

She was on fire, not missing anything. Then Skyler fouled her. It was a bad foul. Jasmine did not complain. She had made-up her mind that she would not complain. No more trash talking. She thought to herself, "I will plainly let my game speak for me. Conserve my talking energy for making my buzzer beating buckets."

Well, the run was almost over when Coach had Lillie guard Jasmine. This time Lillie was more dominant than before. After her performance, she earned a little more of Jasmine's respect. They finished up and went to the shower. When Lillie and Jasmine walked back to their dorm room, Jasmine asked Lillie, "Would you like to do more training together?"

Lillie said, "Yes that would be nice. Two freshmen starters would be helping each other."

More to the point, Jasmine said, "Lillie we have to

put a little more muscle on you."

"Yeah, I need to do that Jasmine. I have always been very thin. I'm glad that we are on the same team."

"Likewise. So, Lillie what part of South Carolina are you from?"

"I'm from Sumpter. What about you?"

"I'm from Monroeville?"

"Never heard of Monroeville."

"Never heard of Sumpter. We got a heavy day tomorrow. Let's get something to eat and call it a night."

"I'm with you Jasmine."

On their way to grab a bite to eat, Jasmine got a text from River. "Have you eaten Jasmine? If not, let's get something to eat. I am starving. I feel like I would like to get a hamburger."

Jasmine responded, "Yes, I have my roommate with me. Meet us at the hamburger place on the corner near the location where I ran into you."

"On the way." River confirmed.

Jasmine, Lillie, and River had a great time. The food was delicious for three hungry people. They all talked freely.

River asked Lillie, "How tall are you?"

"I'm six one."

"Six one? I am six two. I was six two at sixteen years old. How long have you been six one Lillie?"

"Since I was fifteen years old."

"Amazing! Do you like to dance?"

"Yes River. I love dancing. I actually dance better than I play basketball."

"I love to dance too. My girlfriend thought that I was silly wanting to dance professionally."

"Are you serious? I would have preferred a dance scholarship rather than a basketball scholarship."

"Really? Me too! Listen to this."

River knew that if Lillie had dancing in her bones, nothing would stop her from moving when she heard this song. He touched a button. *Get Up Offa That*

Thing by James Brown came on. Lillie jumped up and started dancing. She moved like she did not have a bone in her body. Nothing but smoothness. Then, River jumped up and started dancing with her. Their joy was contagious, so much so, that many who were in the burger shop got up and started dancing.

Jasmine knew her cousin well. At that moment, she knew that Marylou was out of the picture. Those two danced so hard. Jasmine could not bring herself to end it all. As soon as they would take a break, someone else would play an upbeat dance song. It went on for hours. So, instead of getting a quick bite to eat and returning to the dorm to get some sleep, they stayed at the burger shop until about ten p.m., four hours longer than expected.

Chapter 17

River sent a text to Jasmine early the next morning. He said he had a wonderful time but needed to talk as soon as possible.

"What is it River?"

"I have some free time today. Can you meet now for breakfast?"

"I'm getting up. Remember you danced all

night long with Lillie. I was hoping to sleep in and go running later."

"Please Jasmine!"

"Okay. Twenty minutes. Meet you in the

cafeteria."

"Thanks Jasmine. See you in twenty minutes."

Jasmine felt that he wanted to talk about Lillie. She

saw it in River's eyes the night before. When Lillie asked where she was going, Jasmine told her that she was going to have breakfast with River. Lillie asked if she could tag along. Not wanting to embarrass River or Lillie, Jasmine said, "It's some family business he probably wants to talk about. So maybe next time."

"No problem, Jasmine. Please tell River hello."

"Will do Lillie. See you later."

When Jasmine arrived at the cafeteria, River was already sitting at the table. Jasmine walked over and asked, "What's going on River?"

River answered, "Let's go through the line to get our food first."

Jasmine had never seen River act like that. She reasoned that it must have been something more than what she originally thought. They finished eating in no time. Afterwards, they began to talk.

River said, "Marylou called me very early this morning. She was rambling at first, then she told me she couldn't see me anymore."

Jasmine asked, "Maybe that was why she didn't say anything to me about you coming to Alabama to study journalism. That makes sense."

"No Jasmine. Let me start from the beginning. You know a long time ago, she found out that you and I were cousins."

"Yes, I remember that. She was over the top angry."

"She was Jasmine. But she was curious how I knew so much about our family history. She wanted to know more about her family history also. Well, she never did because she went to Mobile for the summer and then again the next summer."

"Yes, I know that River."

"Okay what you don't know is that she met a person that knew her momma. This person asked how Mrs. Marshall was doing. Marylou asked her how she knew her momma. She went on to tell Marylou that she knew the lady who adopted her. Marylou told her momma what the lady said. Both of them went crazy. Mrs. Marshall did not know that she was adopted."

Jasmine interrupted, "Whoa! So why did she not know that? Oh, my goodness! How is Marylou doing?"

"Marylou is doing okay now. But her momma was so distraught that she could not rest until she could talk to the lady that Marylou had spoken too. Time passed. Then this morning, Marylou called to tell me her momma got all kinds of records and information from ancestry. She found out who was her real momma and daddy."

"Is it anyone I know?"

"You do not know this person Neither do I know this person because she does not live in Monroeville. She lives in Mobile."

"River we know plenty of people in Mobile because our family, who originally came from France, settled in Mobile before moving to Monroeville."

"Who is it River?"

"It's your grandmother's sister."

"My grandmother's sister? She gave Mrs. Marshall up for adoption. Why?"

"I don't know."

"So, Marylou and I are related. That's it?"

"Okay, I know it's early in the morning. Jasmine, if you and I are related, then Marylou and I are related."

"Not good. Not good at all. Really River? Oh my. Incredible! I am so happy I did not bring Lillie. This is show-nuf an unexpected revelation. I thought you wanted to talk to me about Lillie. The funny thing is that I told her you probably wanted to talk about our family business. She wanted to eat breakfast with us. I told her next time. Also, she asked me to tell you hello."

"Jasmine, this is fresh news. I do not think your momma knows yet. Why don't you give her a call before you call Marylou?"

"I will call momma now. I have to go River. I will

talk to you later today." Jasmine needed privacy before she could talk to her momma, so she sprinted to her room. Lillie was not there when Jasmine burst into the room. She quickly dialed her momma.

"Momma, I found out that Marylou's momma was adopted. Her real momma is grandmomma's sister who I do not know. Did you know that?"

"Sure. I knew a little bit about it."

"What do you mean 'a little bit about it?'"

"I knew Missy was adopted."

"How long have you known that?"

"I guess since before I met your daddy."

"Why the big secret? Why didn't you tell Mrs. Marshall?"

"Baby, it was so complicated?"

"What else haven't you told me?

"Well, a few things I have not told you."

"Please tell me something momma."

"Okay Jasmine. Remember when you were questioning me so much because I would not go out on a date with Coach Van Damme?"

"Yes, momma I remember. He was not trying to marry you. It was a date. That is all. That's what I remember."

"Yes, that's true. It is time you know a little more about why. Remember I told you I knew a person who had to leave town because of dating a white man?"

"Yes, momma I remember. Please! Just spit it out. Please momma. This is driving me insane."

"Ok. That person was your grandmomma's sister, your great Aunt. She's Missy's real momma. I heard about it when I was maybe thirteen or fourteen years old. To sum it up, I never wanted to talk about what happened or experience that because I saw how that incident traumatized the family."

"So, did you ever meet her?"

"Yes, she is still alive, living in Mobile."

"Momma, so you knew that River was related to Marylou?"

"No, honey I really didn't think about it. This story happened so long ago. Nobody talked about it. It escaped my memory, tucked away neatly in my brain. I only recalled bits and pieces. Remember, my marriage and children consumed my young mind."

"So, you and Mrs. Marshall are first cousins?"

"Yes, I guess so. I have never been good with that. I would say we are cousins. I am so sorry you seem disturbed by this uncovered story. It should not change your relationship with Marylou."

"No, you are right. However, it will affect Marylou's relationship with River. She broke up with him today."

"You are absolutely right. Maybe you, Marylou and River can forgive me."

"Well momma, you are forgetting about Mrs. Marshall. She is your best friend."

"We have already talked about it. She understands that I was an overwhelmed teen who could not tell the story because my momma had forbidden me to do so. Then I forgot all about it. Can you understand that? Can you put yourself in my shoes? If not, I am sorry you cain't do that."

"Sure. I can try to do so momma. I am so sorry. This has just stirred me emotionally. I never expected that to happen. Momma is there anything else you haven't told me?"

"Yes, since we talked about Coach Van Damme, the news at the spa is that he married the lady that your daddy went out on a date with two times. She was two-timing your daddy from the first date."

"Well, it never stops. You have so many secrets."

"Jasmine, let me tell you something. These are not my secrets. These secrets belong to others. I am not the kind of person that wants to be a busybody in another person's relationships. You know that and yet you are upset with me? No doubt your daddy knows. Did he tell you?"

"No, he didn't momma. You are right. According to River, Marylou seems to be okay with everything.

Mrs. Marshall is doing better. I think River will be okay now that he has met my roommate, who loves to dance with him. Actually, they had a dance off at the burger shop last night."

"Jasmine, thanks for telling me that. You have made me feel better. I am sorry this upset you so, my little baby girl. Other than that, how are you doing?"

"I'm doing okay. I am happy that River will be going to Alabama with me. It would be good to see a familiar face. Skyler is a little jealous of River. I have not told him yet, that River is my cousin."

"Jasmine since you blasted me for keeping a secret that I had no control over because momma instructed me not to disclose it, how is it that you have kept this secret from Skyler? Do you think that is a double standard?"

"Momma, I can see now how it is so easy to be a hypocrite. You are so right. I was purposely trying to play with his feelings. Not good. Thank you for bringing that to my attention."

Cashmere said, "I get what you were trying to do, but as you can see, that is a double standard. There is a principle involved. You wrongly applied to me that keeping a secret was bad and you teasingly applied keeping a secret by toying with someone's heart as perhaps cute. What if he did that to you? Does that make sense?"

"Momma, it makes perfect sense. I will correct that as soon as I can."

"Good baby girl. Moving on. Breaking news for Sam and Malinda. They want a real simple wedding with the two of them during your winter break. Will that work for you?"

"That will absolutely work for me. I am sure the wedding will be beautiful. I knew they had potential job offers. So that's cool momma. Do I have to do anything other than show up for the wedding?"

"That's it. If you would like to bring a guest, let me know? I am starting to pull the guest list together. Wanted you to know that Malinda wants to invite

Tommy and his parents since they have been neighbors for almost twenty years."

"How does Sam feel about that?"

"Sam is okay. He does not feel threatened. As a matter of fact, he encouraged her to invite Tommy and his parents. Your brother is a wonderful young man. I'm not saying that because he is my son."

"I know momma. Will daddy attend the wedding? Will you sit together?"

"He said that he will attend the wedding. We will do our best to present a unified front for Sam. It is the least that we can do. You know, your daddy had the choice to bring another guest it he wanted to; but he declined the offer. I am not bringing anyone. Should not be a problem. So, there you have it."

"Well momma, I'm glad I called you. That was a lot of stuff to catch up on. Please tell Sam and Malinda that I am happy for them. Please give me the date as soon as possible."

"I will definitely let you know as soon as I can.

Who would you like to bring?"

"I'm not sure yet. I might bring my roommate. Not even sure if Skyler would be interested in coming. How many guests can I bring?"

"How many do you want to bring?"

"Maybe Skyler and my roommate."

"I don't think that would be a problem. No, it will not be a problem. Please let me know if you want to bring more of your friends to the wedding."

"Thanks Momma. That will work. I'll talk to you later."

Jasmine hung up the phone and headed out the door to find River. As she turned the corner, she bumped into Skyler. There would be no more excuses. She had to talk to Skyler.

Chapter 18

As Jasmine was locking the door to her room, Skyler shouted, "Hey Jasmine. Where are you headed so fast?"

"Hey Skyler. I'm on my way to see River."

"River? What's up with River?"

"I need to tell him something."

"Can you call him?"

"I could. But I wanted to talk face to face."

"I thought we could go for a walk."

"A walk? Not now Skyler. I'll see you later."

Skyler was feeling jittery. He had not met River. He was concerned that he had not been forthright with Jasmine about his feelings. After that, now someone else was getting her attention. So, without an invitation, Skyler said this quickly, "I'm going with you Jasmine."

"Ok. No problem, Skyler. Let's go."

Skyler was so surprised that Jasmine agreed to let him go along with her to see River. He was happy plus very much interested in finding out why it was so important to see River in person. When they found River, he was sitting quietly with Lillie in the library. Now Skyler understood that it would have been very difficult to talk on the phone at the library. Skyler was thrilled that he insisted he would go along with Jasmine. Although he was thinking that River was a threat, that cleared up once he saw River with Lillie. Jasmine motioned for River to come outside. River told Lillie that he would be right back.

Jasmine said, "Hey River. To begin with, I got off the phone with momma a little while ago. She explained to me everything that happened so there is nothing to worry about. I see that you are with Lillie; therefore, I will not keep you long. Oh, let me introduce you to Skyler. Skyler this is River, my special long-time friend." Skyler's heart dropped.

"Yes Skyler, River is my special friend. My special cousin." Skyler was relieved to hear that report. Jasmine kept her word that she would tell Skyler as soon as possible that she and River were cousins. However, she did not go into details about it, nor why she was wrong for not telling him sooner. It did not phase Skyler one bit that she could have told him earlier. Somehow, he simply felt relieved that now he knew who River was and that he was not a threat to their relationship.

He did not hesitate to say, "Hey River, good to meet you man. I thought I was going to have a little competition for my girl. I'm so thankful."

River said, "Hey Skyler. I heard about you when Jasmine went to Sarasota-Bradenton for a basketball camp a few years ago. Good to finally meet you."

Skyler said, "Yeah Man. Good to finally meet you too."

River asked, "Jasmine what is the news from home?"

"It's a lot of news River. The main news is that Sam and Malinda are going to get married in a couple of months. It will not be a large wedding, just the two of them. All we have to do is show up. Momma said we can bring a guest or a few of our classmates if we want to do so."

"Good, I will ask Lillie to go with me."

"Ok River. I will let momma know. You probably need to ask Lillie before I tell momma."

"Will do cuz. Skyler are you coming man?"

"Absolutely. I would like to go River. You know that I have to get an invitation first."

"Skyler would you like to go with me?" Jasmine asked.

"Yes, I would. I wish my dad could come because he needs a little break too."

"Oh, that would be perfect Skyler. My family would like that. Ask him. I will let momma know."

"I will."

River said, "Jasmine I need to get back to the Library. I really like Lillie. I will ask her if she would like to come. Will confirm with you later."

Skyler was finally able to put the pieces together. He was so excited to receive an invitation from Jasmine. Not only that, he received an invitation to a wedding, along with the fact that he had continued to speak of marrying Jasmine one day.

After walking Jasmine back to her dorm room, Skyler asked, "Jasmine would you like to marry me one day?"

"Skyler, I don't know because I have been so consumed with playing basketball. Maybe one day I will think about marriage, but not now."

"I don't want you to get away from me. I want you to promise me that you will give me a chance to show you that I would make a good husband."

"I don't even know what a good wife or husband would be. I only want to play basketball."

"You can play basketball. I'm talking about a little later."

"Skyler, you don't even know me. Sometimes I don't even know me. Why are you so interested in marriage?"

"Because I saw how in love my parents were. I wanted that one day. Although my parents divorced, it was not because they did not love each other. They worked different schedules in different cities. Eventually, they stopped spending quality time with each other."

"Skyler, my parents were teenage sweethearts. I found out recently that my momma was an athlete and gave it up. They were so young. So much in love until they had their first baby; then, their love dwindled. How can you stop loving your spouse because you have a baby? So, I made up my mind to follow my dream, be happy with that. After that, maybe later in life get married, if at all."

"Jasmine, I'm willing to believe that your parents

still love each other, just like my parents. They are afraid to try again because of the hurt. I am willing to take that chance. I have learned a great deal from examining their lives. They are older but neither one is willing to express their mistakes to each other and reunite. I believe that two good forgivers are what makes a successful marriage. Neither one of my parents was a good forgiver. I believe with all my heart that I would work very hard to keep my family together, even if I had to make serious sacrifices because when you love someone, you should be willing to die for them."

"Skyler, do you believe in love at first sight?"

"No Jasmine. I believe in strong chemistry at first sight. I believed that when I saw you at fifteen years old, I liked your sweetness, your innocence, and your simplicity. Your looks along with your physique were secondary. Why do you think I chased you down at the airport?"

"I have never had a boyfriend, especially one that

is interested in marriage. I positively do not want to follow in my parents' footsteps. Does that make sense Skyler? It seems like their pain was so much deeper than their love."

"Believe me Jasmine, talk to your momma. She will honestly share with you what happened. More than that, she will probably tell you what she could have changed if you ask her. I have done that with my momma. That is how I know. I will not pressure you right now. Talk to her for me. And after talking to her, and you find out marriage was the worst mistake she could have made, I will table my interest in marriage to you. Will you do that for me? No, will you do that for you?"

"For me?"

"Yes, for you. You cannot allow your parents' divorce to frighten you from ever enjoying the wonderful gift of marriage. That is a gift from God. Remember the Almighty is the originator of marriage."

"How are you able to talk like an old man when you are only a couple of years older than me?"

"I have thought about marriage since I was a little boy. I have kept myself pure for my wife. I prayed to the Creator to help me find one. He has answered my prayer. I am not sure how he can convince you, that I'm the one."

"That's really sweet Skyler. I will talk to my momma. I will do my best to understand that although my parents' marriage failed, I could have a successful marriage."

"That's all I ask now Jasmine. That's all I ask."

"I have never had very deep conversations with my momma. Her hurt seemed to have run so deep until I could not bring myself to ask her anything more. But I promise I will. I never would have imagined that you had this really serious side to you Skyler. I considered you to be a young man that was teasing me about marriage. I will be nineteen years old in about eight months. That is when momma had her first child. But do not worry, I will talk to momma."

"Thanks Jasmine. I am light-hearted; but I am a very serious-minded person. I have strong beliefs in having a strong united family. So have a good night's sleep. I will talk with you later." As he reached over to give her a hug, the same light hug he had given her before, Jasmine leaned over and kissed him lightly on the lips. Skyler was frozen. There was a brief silence. Neither he nor Jasmine said anything. It seemed like hours, as it was only seconds when Jasmine asked, "Did I do something wrong Skyler?"

"No, you didn't do anything wrong. No girl has ever kissed me, let alone on the lips. I have never kissed a girl. I had a strange sensation that overtook my body. I could not move. I have never had that feeling before. A nerve sensation went all the way down my body, from my lips to my toes. And I wanted to experience that again. But why did you kiss me?"

"Well, I honestly don't know. It came over me to

do that. I have never kissed a boy at all either. No boy has kissed me before. I don't know Skyler."

"Jasmine how did you feel when you kissed me?"

"It was intense, even scary. Internally, I was out of control. I felt like I was in a small canoe. A waterfall out of heaven picked me up. Tossed me over a cliff and I landed on your lips.

"Sensational! Anything else?"

"I felt weak. Within seconds, I felt very deep aggressive feelings Skyler. I felt like I was quivering. It was like every nerve in my body was about to explode."

"Jasmine, I'm so happy I had my first kiss with you. Isn't that wonderful to share?

"I suppose so Skyler."

"How do you feel about what happened?"

I had not planned to kiss you on your lips at all. I barely touched your lips with my lips. I really think it was the way you spoke to me. It was so kind. Tender. Your tone of voice woke me up and endeared me to you even more. Your words produced another dimension to our relationship. You looked at me totally different when you approached me to hug me. Maybe it was your warm hazel eyes that appeared so attentive, so comforting. Your presence was beautiful. To think how wonderfully made you are makes me ponder why you would be so interested in me, a Southern country girl from Monroeville, Alabama."

"Not only am I interested in you, I'm fascinated with you. You are innocent, yet smart. You have goals. You are focused. You are naturally beautiful. You do not even know it. Your smile is tantalizing. You are giving. You care about others. Your statue is strong, but graceful. I have not met another person that I would like to spend my entire life with other than you, even if it were at the cost of not playing professional basketball. That is how much I need you. How much I want you in my life."

"Skyler, would you do that for me? Sacrifice a

career that you dreamed about?"

"Jasmine, I have wanted a wife long before I wanted to play professional basketball. I would hug my pillow at night, with the hopes of one day, cuddling my wife instead of a pillow."

"That is noble Skyler; but I would never want you to give up your dream. We have been buddies, speaking to each other like fellow athletes for over three years. I see you as the man that could be my husband. The reality of that is overwhelming. For a moment I felt like you. Basketball left my heart. I wanted to marry you today. It seemed like only you were what I needed, what I wanted. I was thinking, 'Am I being realistic?' Although, I had not been looking for love, I feel that I have found it with you in this short time.

"You have helped me to see, what I could not see, perhaps what was in the crevice of my heart, in the back of my mind. The words you spoke to me are undeniably words I will cherish. You have taught me in a short conversation something I did not know about myself. I am excited about that.

"It was almost like you were writing poetry for me, words that no one had ever said to me before. I felt all mushy. I am not a romantic, fantasy type of girl. But with you I could be, because within one conversation, I was there. So how can I be a tough athlete at the same time be a mushy woman? Seems highly impossible."

"You can Jasmine. I have confidence in you. You can be anything you want with me. I love you just like you are, along with, what you can become."

"Surprising Skyler. This conversation is blowing my mind. You can marry any young woman that you want. You have made me feel like you only want me. That I am one in a billion. That I am extraordinary. You make me feel beautiful, even though I have never thought of myself as beautiful, primarily as an athlete. You have surprised me with feelings that you are not embarrassed to express to me. And I believe you.

You are far from being a typical twenty-year-old. Now, I have so much more to talk to momma about. Will that embarrass you?"

"Not at all Jasmine. I could talk to you all night because I have so much more that I have kept waiting for the right time. But we really need to get some rest, so I'll talk to you tomorrow." He took her hand, placed it on his heart and said, "This is how my heart beats every time I see you. It races. I get jittery.

"When I saw you with River, I secretly prayed that he would disappear. I have found a good thing with you. I do not want to let you go. Please believe me." Skyler waved goodbye. Jasmine hugged him tightly.

Shortly after that hug she said, "I don't want to let you go." But she released him and went into her room, closing the door behind her.

Neither slept well that night because the relationship had changed with a simple kiss.

Chapter 19

River and Jasmine met for breakfast, seeing that they both had so much to talk about, even though, they concluded at breakfast that neither one of them was truly hungry. Jasmine told him everything that she had talked to her momma about the night before. River was really happy everything worked out. She also told him that she and Skyler had a very deep conversation about marriage. Much to her surprise, River said the same thing about Lillie, that they talked a very long time about marriage.

Within five minutes of their conversation, Lillie walked into the cafeteria and a minute or so after that, Skyler walked in too. They all sat together.

Unpredictably, they all had turned to a different juncture in their life. Not knowing how to talk about the night before left them all somewhat shy. So, River broke his silence by asking, "How is basketball going Skyler?"

"It's going good River. Cain't complain. You know my dad is the coach."

"I feel you man. No need to ruffle any feathers."

"Yeah River, I'm really looking forward to getting to know you a little better. You have a great cousin that I love. I'm looking forward to loving her for the rest of my life."

Jasmine bobbed her head for a second and jumped right in. "I'm thrilled to learn more about you as well Skyler." Skyler smiled at her. Jasmine returned the smile. Besides that, River could not believe how shy Jasmine looked to be. Jasmine caught River looking at her with a perplexed face.

Then Jasmine said, "River and Lillie, Skyler has a serious side that I did not know until last night."

"Hey! I have been trying to show her, but she kept running away from me. I had to hunt her down on several occasions to talk to her. By the way, I really want to talk with your dad and your mom. Remember when your mom and I played a trick on you?

"Yeah. I remember that."

"Can I talk to your parents?"

"Yes Skyler. Why don't the four of us go to Monroeville in a couple of weeks. That will give momma time to get everything set up for us. We can talk with Sam and Malinda also. Lillie and I can stay with momma; while you and River can stay with daddy."

"Jasmine, I don't know if Lillie and I should go. Do you think Marylou will feel left out?"

"No, she is fine River. I think Tommy is keeping her busy."

"You didn't tell me that." River mentioned.

"Sorry River. Not sure if anything will come out

of it."

Skyler stated, "Hey Jasmine. That would be great if we all went together for a weekend. I have not asked my dad yet if he wants to go to attend the wedding. Maybe I should wait until our visit to Monroeville."

"That's okay with me Skyler. Momma would love a visit. I will call her tonight to tell her. I will also tell my daddy too."

They all left, going into different directions. Each one went about the day as usual. Sometime during the day, Skyler slipped back to Jasmine's dorm, then slid under her door, an envelope with his first poem to her. The title of the poem was *What is Your Name?*

What is Your Name?

I saw you in Sarasota-Bradenton
In a city full of well-known champions
Attending a basketball camp
I saw a beautiful girl running down the ramp
An explosive girl with a dynamite game

Yet she would not give me her name
I discovered that she was flying to Mobile
When I drove my car with an empty gas tank to fill
I ran through the airport to find out her name
When I bumped into the girl who had me going insane
To my surprise she looked dead into my eye
And said my man all I have to say is goodbye
I yelled again what is your name
She said wouldn't you like to know
Jasmine my man

Although Skyler spoke poetic words to Jasmine the night before, which sent her into another world, he hoped that she would appreciate the words he wrote quickly to show his sincere heart. Far more than that, it would be the first poem that she would have ever received from anyone.

Skyler was able to get to his class on time and have a pleasant day. When he got to the gym for basketball practice, his daddy was busy talking to some of the players. The cheerleaders were on the other side of the gym having a meeting. Instead of going to suit up, Skyler walked over to his daddy and in a calm voice said, "Daddy, I need to talk to you."

"What's up son?"

"Jasmine's brother is getting married during the winter break, not sure of the exact date, but Jasmine wanted to invite you to go with us. I should have asked you earlier, so you could plan for it."

Skyler was surprised to hear that his daddy would not be able to attend the wedding. He did not give Skyler a detailed reason, other than he was going to visit a long-time friend that he had not seen in a while. He also said that the friend had been having some health challenges and needed the encouragement. Skyler did not pressure him. He told his daddy that they were getting serious.

"Serious?" asked his dad. Serious like dating or serious like doing something else."

"Daddy, so that you know, we are serious about dating and eventually getting married."

"Son, do you think that you two are ready for

marriage?"

"Not exactly but looking forward to it. We are getting to know each other better. Daddy I knew I was going to marry her when I met her in Sarasota-Bradenton."

"I didn't know that you felt that way so long ago. That was a few years ago."

"Yes daddy. I told her that I was going to marry her one day. But last night, she really believed me. She originally thought I had been teasing her."

"What about basketball?"

"For sure, we are going to keep focused on basketball as we prepare for marriage."

"Son, I'm sure she is a nice girl. But there will be others. Look at those cheerleaders over there. One or all of them could be interested in you. See there. Look over there how they are looking at you."

"They can look all they want. Not one of them is for me. I have found who I want to marry. I am focused. Jasmine is too. And we have similar goals.

I don't want to play pro basketball if she is not in my life."

"Son, don't you think you are carrying this a little too far? You don't mean that."

"The truth daddy is that I do mean it. Besides that, I am not looking for groupies. I am young. I know that Jasmine is young, and she is not looking for groupies. I told her that we cannot let our parents failed marriage frighten us. We have to learn from their mistakes. Would you like to help me learn from your mistakes?"

"Yes, I don't mind. But now is not the time."

"I get it dad. Practice has not started yet. I did not want another day to pass without telling you my intentions. We understand there will be challenges; particularly, like there are challenges in every aspect of life, even basketball. But neither one of us is preparing to run away from problems. We might be innocent, but not blind. It is okay that you are concerned. And I hope you turn your concerns into helping me to become a more responsible man and husband."

"Skyler, my son, I'm not going to doom you to failure. You are right. My experiences in life should be lessons shared with you of what I did wrong. Ok. Let's continue to work on helping you to set a good foundation for your future marriage."

"Thanks daddy. I need your advice as I work hard to be the best person I can be."

"Son go get dressed. Let's play some basketball."

The school hired a women's basketball coach. Jasmine would not be playing with Skyler during the practice as much. Lots of changes.

At the end of the day, Jasmine got back to her dorm room where she found the envelope with the poem that Skyler had written to her. She cracked up when she read it. She thought to herself, "I have met a very well-rounded young man." Now she had something else she needed to tell her momma.

When Jasmine settled in, she called her momma.

"Hey momma. I do not know where to start. I want to come home in two weeks with Skyler and River and my roommate Lillie. She is now dating River."

"What's the purpose of the trip?"

"Momma, Skyler and I are talking about marriage. You know he has been telling me for almost three years that he was going to marry me one day. Yesterday he was so serious that I believed him. He wants to talk to you and daddy. I thought that the boys could stay with daddy. The girls could stay with you. Would you check with daddy for me on that?"

"You know that I have always liked Skyler from the day he wanted to make sure that you got his momma's hope chest because she did not have any daughters."

"Yeah, he brought up the same thing. I really want to talk to you about marriage. We will not be getting married soon though. I just want to know what I should be aware of, how to prepare for a whole new married life and especially I need to know these things if either or both of us are going to play professional basketball. I have so much to tell you. So, when I get there, I really want to listen more to you. Will that be okay momma?"

"Honey that sounds exciting. Both of my children are really growing up. You have surprised me. Sam too. I thought you were not interested in marriage."

"I thought so too momma. But when Skyler was about to hug me, I kissed him on the lip. It is like that one kiss changed my mine. I was not sure why I did that. But he had talked to me in such a kind yet serious manner. I could tell he had been thinking about me for a long time. As he talked, I analyzed my feelings. I had to admit, I felt the same. I was hiding behind the basketball. Does that make sense?"

"Sure, it does my dear. I will help you by answering any and all of your questions when you come for a visit. I would be delighted to talk with Skyler. I will ask your daddy if he could put up boys for a weekend. I will call you when I find out what's what. Is that good?"

"Yes, good momma. That is great. I really appreciate that you want to help us understand what all is involved in marriage. I gotta go. I'll talk to you later."

In the meantime, Skyler had finished basketball practice. His daddy asked if they could sit down for dinner and talk. Skyler agreed that would be good. They went back to Coach Chadsworth's apartment to have some leftover baked chicken, rice, and broccoli.

"Dad, is this about playing basketball?"

"No son. This is about giving you some information that I don't think you know."

"Okay, sounds good."

"Skyler when your momma and I got married, we loved each other very much. Our brief conversation about you and Jasmine, made me think about your momma and me. We never had major arguments. We both worked and enjoyed our work. From the beginning, I wish I had done what you are doing, coming to me for advice. Anyway, I got this coaching job that was in Tampa, Florida at a high school.

"Your momma was working in Bradenton at a small school. After we married, we spent a lot of time together, then you were born. During that time, I thought that I needed to get a better job to support our new addition to the family, so I applied for a job in Alabama. As you probably figured out, I did not come home every night because of the distance. Your momma did not want to move to Alabama. For that reason, I came home only on the weekends every other week. Did your momma ever tell you this story?"

"No, daddy I don't remember this story."

"I worked at this high school for about four years. She seemed to be happy when I came home. So, I decided to apply for another coaching job. I applied to Alabama and got the job I have now. It was so exciting. When I came home, I only talked about the school, the game, and things like that. I had become a workaholic. Although we were together when I came home, it wasn't enough."

"In that case daddy, this means that approximately the first five or six years of my life or more, you were living out of state."

"That's right. Seemed like your momma was okay with that. She did not make a big stink about it. Never. Since she was not a complainer, I figured everything was okay. And we could live like this forever or until she complained. That was not sound reasoning. See, I liked my life. I thought she liked her life."

"Did you ever ask her again if she wanted to move to Alabama?"

"No, I didn't. As I mentioned, it seemed like she was happy. So, this particular week, I was going to go home a little later than usual; but your momma seemed disturbed. So, I came on home earlier to see why she was so disturbed. When I walked in, she told me she did not want to be married any longer. She burst into tears. I was trying to figure out what was going on. She rambled for a few minutes. I asked her to slow down and tell me why she wanted to get a divorce. This is what she said, "Luke, I have committed adultery. I cain't live with you anymore."

"Skyler do you know what adultery is?"

"Yes, it's when someone in the marriage has done something wrong."

"Yes, you are partially correct. It's when a marriage mate has sex with someone that is not your spouse."

"Momma did that?"

"Yes."

"Do you know with who she did that?"

"With her co-worker."

"No way daddy. I do not believe you. Momma would never have done that to you."

"Skyler, I'm sorry you don't believe me. But it is true. I did not blame your momma for that at all. She was lonely. She was in a pseudo marriage, meaning that it looked like we were married, but we were not living together. It was marriage on paper, but not in person. I was not there for her emotionally, mentally, spiritually, and sexually. That put her in an awkward position.

"Her co-worker tried to spend time with her to encourage her. She became emotionally attached to him. He became emotionally attached to her. They went to lunch together every day. He called her when he had problems. Obviously, she was confiding in him about me, instead of confiding in me. Once that happened, it was easier to have a sexual relationship. And that sexual relationship broke her down. There might be more to the story; but that is what she told me son. One day she might be willing to tell you the whole story.

"Although I forgave her as soon as she told me. I never asked, 'Why did you do this?' I knew why. Anyway, she was so devastated by that one mistake, she was never mentally stable again. This is what I want you to know about some women. When they do wrong, they may not reconcile their feelings for weeks, months or even years later. It has been over ten years since that has happened with your momma. She has not been able to resolve her feelings at all. It caused her to have a nervous breakdown last year."

"Dad, she hid her nervous breakdown from me. How was she able to do that?"

"Love. She cares about you so much that she wanted to do anything she could to help you out. She loves you. You are the fruitage of her belly."

"I visited Liz two times over the past year; ever since, she checked herself into the mental institution. During the winter break, I had arranged to visit her for a longer period of time. I do not think I can do that now with the basketball schedule. If she would accept me back, I would marry her right away. Her condition does not bother me. I love her. She still loves me. I wish I could turn back the hands of time; however, the pain is honestly too great for her."

"Daddy I did not know all of this had happened. All I saw was that you two loved each other. That is what I told Jasmine. So, daddy, what can I do?"

"First of all, when you get married, be present. Never take your wife for granted. Do not be selfish. Look after her interests as they were your very own. Make sacrifices. Never assume that everything is all right. Communicate about little things, big things. So as much as we loved each other, I did not nurture my wife. I removed the circumstances for her to nurture me. Treat your wife like she is so important to you that, living without her is paramount to death. Do you need me to tell you more?"

"No. Thank you, daddy. Do you think that if I talk to momma it would help?"

"Son, I don't want to take a chance that your knowing what happened would hurt her worse or possibly kill her."

"What a dilemma daddy. What a predicament. I hope that I can go to see her when you return or at least call her while you are there. I know she would like to hear from Jasmine. Momma is uniquely so sweet. I hate to see her suffer like that. But then I will take to heart everything you have told me. That has broken my heart daddy. How long will she be there at the mental institution?"

"The doctors don't no. Her progress has been so slow. It is really up to her. She has to forgive herself."

"I told you this after being divorced ten years, in order that you should consider your wife's feelings with every decision you make."

"Daddy, you have done what I wanted you to do for me. Do you think that momma would have advice for me too?"

"Sure, she will. Do not bring up this subject unless she brings it up. I am not sure how she will react. When you talk to her, do as you always have done."

"Thank you. This is unbelievably shocking."

What Skyler's parents kept from him actually made him question if they were really in love. And the only way to find out was to hear his momma's side of the story. Could she handle the interrogation without added stress? Seeing his momma now became a priority.

Chapter 20

Cashmere called her ex-husband to find out if he could host the young men for a weekend. Immediately, she called Jasmine to let her know that Geronimo could not host the boys in two weeks. It would have to be the coming weekend. Geronimo wanted to put together a little cookout for everyone including Sam and Malinda. Following the cookout, he wanted to take the boys to play billiards. Cashmere wanted to treat the girls to facials or massages once they came.

She told Jasmine that they could have a full weekend together if they could come down Friday evening and leave Sunday afternoon. Three couples that were interested in marriage would be talking to a couple that had been divorced for five years. About the time Cashmere finished the call with her momma, she received a text from Skyler. He asked if she had a good day. He asked, if possible, could she talk for a little while. She said yes. And they met at the library.

As soon as Jasmine arrived, she noticed that Skyler was already there. She was thinking about the poem and wanted to share what her thoughts were about his poem; however, he had a very serious look on his face as she approached him. When she smiled at him, the dent between his brows eased a little. He presented her with a smile. Not the usual smile. She knew something was on his mind.

"Skyler, you look very serious. Are you doing ok?"

"Yes, I'm ok Jasmine. I had the most intense conversation with my daddy. I tell you; I'm still trying to process everything." As he related in detail what his daddy had discussed, Jasmine squinted her eyes, raised her shoulders, and ducked her head. Then she moved back from him as if she had seen something that made her squirm. She could not believe it.

"Skyler, that's horrible! No, not your momma, the one who gave me the hope chest. Oh no! How are you doing, now that you have learned what really happened with your parents?"

"I'm wrestling with that. I always thought that they loved each other; but the missing link was why they did not stay married. They really hid many things from me. My momma undoubtedly had a nervous breakdown trying to conceal it from me. Just think, when she gave you the hope chest, she seemed so supportive of marriage. I'm especially trying to figure out the feelings behind her actions."

"Skyler don't try to figure it out. It seems like I received the gift because she loved you. Or maybe because you talked about me. It was a friendly gesture. I was honored to receive it; but at the time, the handmade hope chest that momma had given to me touched my heart. Besides that, she never had one, so it worked out when I gave it to her."

"Yes, you are probably right Jasmine. But what I believe is that she loved my dad so much, she felt that being with him would remind her constantly of what she had done."

"Maybe one day, she will tell you what happened from her perspective. Don't you think so?"

"Maybe she will tell you Jasmine. I'm almost sure she will one day."

"I'm really sad for you Skyler. Maybe this will cheer you up a little. My daddy wants us to come this weekend. Would that be ok?"

"Sure. The sooner the better. Will River and Lillie be able to go?"

"I got off the phone with momma moments before you texted me. Look over there Skyler. It is River and Lillie. Let's ask them now."

"Hey River. Daddy said we would have to come this weekend. They are planning a few things for us. Would that be okay for you and Lillie?" Lillie nodded yes as she looked at River."

River said, "Yes that's fine. What time do you think we should leave?"

"Well, what about after our last class on Friday?" Lillie responded.

"So around three o'clock?" Jasmine asked.

All agreed. Lillie and Jasmine walked back to their dorm room together. While they were studying, Lillie asked, "Do you really think that River likes me?"

"I do Lillie."

"Well, why did River ask about Marylou?"

"Lillie, it's really crazy. They liked each other; but nothing serious came out of it because she went to Mobile for a while. The short of it is that they found out Marylou's momma is related to me and River. He did not want her to feel awkward."

"Whew! That threw me when I heard him ask about Marylou. I did not know all of that. Thank you for explaining that to me."

As Jasmine smiled, she said, "Lillie, the truth is that River likes you a lot. How do you feel about him?"

"I like him a lot too. Do you think it was too soon to talk about marriage?"

"Well, it's on the minds of most Southern girls. Since you asked me, it is good to talk about it so that we can have a good understanding of what is involved in marriage. I mean like the day-to-day things that each spouse has to be concerned with. We should not accept the storybook view that marriage is all about romance. And the ending is that they lived happily ever after. I'm sure we know from living at home that there is a lot more involved."

"Jasmine, my parents have only talked to me about basketball. I feel that it's more to life than basketball."

"Well Lillie, I would have fit in your family because that is all I want to talk about. Since I have met Skyler, he talked about marriage so much until I am not afraid of it anymore. I like basketball, but I used it as an escape. I'm learning that my parents' marriage does not mean that I would have the same problems with marriage."

"Jasmine, that is so cool. I am so happy that we are roommates. We can help each other stay balanced."

"Yeah. Me too. I am really looking forward to going to Monroeville. This will also be a test-run for my parents, especially with Sam and Malinda getting married in a couple of months."

"How do you think they will act Jasmine?"

"I know that they will be civil. I will be looking for the feelings behind the subject of marriage. Skyler is now concerned if his parents were putting on an act after his dad gave him some disturbing news. He was right about his father's love but not so sure now about his momma's love. I'm excited to see if he is right about my parents, that they are still in love."

"Did your parents argue a lot?"

"No, not that I remember Lillie. I remember that they worked all the time."

"My parents ran track. Ninety-nine percent of the time, they had this competitive approach when we had projects in school. At home they used track terms when talking to us."

"Like what?"

"Jasmine like, 'Don't forget to pass the baton.' Or if my siblings and I had a challenge in school, they would say something like this, 'you got to attack that hurdle.'" Lillie started laughing. She could not stop laughing. Then Jasmine started laughing. They laughed for the longest time.

Then Lillie got silly with it. She stood in front of Jasmine and asked, "Who has this posture?"

Jasmine responded, "A hurdler getting ready to jump over the hurdle."

Lillie said, "Your turn."

Jasmine ran to the door, picked up the umbrella, placed it behind her back and asked, "What is this?"

"It's the baton. Pass the baton."

"This is the last one Jasmine. What is this pose?" Jasmine could not figure it out because Lillie was so tall and lanky.

So, Jasmine asked, "Give me a hint."

"It's a trophy that only guy's get."

"Only what guy's get?"

"Do you give up Jasmine?"

"Yes, I cain't imagine. Please another clue."

"Football players get it."

"Not the Heisman?"

"Yep. You looked like a swimmer getting ready to do a tilted cannonball from the high dive."

They laughed so hard until tears dropped from their eyes.

Chapter 21

The big day had arrived for the two young couples to go to Monroeville, Alabama. They were all excited, happy to get insight as to what marriage stories they would receive. More thought provoking was how would they ask their personal questions.

The drive down was beautiful. Traffic was easy. River drove. He and Skyler sat in the front seats. The girls sat in the back seats. They were chatting away when Skyler yelled, "Is that a crow?"

Jasmine and River started laughing. River said, "Hey city boy that's a buzzard."

"River it's a lot of them! Where are they going?"

"Oh Skyler, there is something down the road they

are going to eat. We'll see soon." River replied.

A short time later, they saw a deer on a fenced road that ran parallel with the expressway. It had to be about seven to ten buzzards hovering around it. Skyler had never seen anything like that in his life.

So, Lillie chimed in, "We see buzzards all the time too when we are traveling in South Carolina."

River said, "We are getting off on Evergreen exit. Then we have about twenty-five miles to go, and we will be in Monroeville, Alabama."

Lillie said, "While surfing the internet, I looked up Monroeville, Alabama and found out that two famous authors were from there. I also saw that there were a lot of actors from Alabama."

"Hmm…don't be surprised Lillie, Jasmine and I might be added to that list, especially when I start writing about this fabulous state and my cousin who plays for the University of Alabama in Tuscaloosa." River boasted.

"Okay River, what did I tell you about bragging?"

"I'm not bragging Jasmine. I'm writing an article for the Monroe Journal in my head."

Jasmine started laughing. "Well don't forget that you would have to write about Skyler and Lillie. Guess what River?"

"What?"

"Wouldn't that be fun if we all made the pros? You would have the inside scoop." Jasmine mentioned.

River followed up with a viewpoint question. "How would each of you feel, if all three of you made the pros?"

"Skyler laughed, "I would go to Disney World."

River corrected him. "No Skyler that is a football joke."

Skyler asked them to consider another possibility.

"Yeah, but cain't we change it to basketball?"

Jasmine replied, "We are tired. Let's get on to Monroeville. I will call momma to let her know that we are not far away. This is so exciting."

Skyler asked, "River can we stop for a bathroom

break before we get to Monroeville?"

"Yeah, let me see. The Walmart is not too far away. We can stop there."

They all decided to go into Walmart. Skyler headed straight for the bathroom, while the others browsed. After a couple of minutes, River headed to the hot food section to get some chicken wings for the group. Jasmine and Lillie were looking at the lotion section. There was another woman in that section. They could see only her back, so they did not pay much attention to her. Then they heard a man's voice who asked, "Honey, how long are you going to be in here?" It was a familiar voice, so Jasmine looked up and over. It was Coach Van Damme.

"Hey Coach."

He looked over to see who was speaking to him.

"Jasmine, how are you doing? Are you back living in Monroeville?"

"No, I brought some of my friends with me to visit momma and daddy."

Coach Van Damme's friend walked up to Jasmine and said, "You look like your daddy Jasmine. I was not able to meet you; but I saw you play before. You are a really good basketball player."

"Thank you." Jasmine replied.

"How is your daddy doing?"

"My daddy is doing fine. My momma is too. I heard that you married coach. Congratulations."

"Yes. Thank you."

"I hope you have a good marriage. We stopped to get some snacks and have a bathroom break. We got to get going. Nice to see you Coach. Take care."

Skyler, River, Lillie, and Jasmine headed for the door. When they got into the car, they felt a little more refreshed. The couple of chicken wings that River had gotten for each of them hit the spot until they could have a full meal with the family. They were back on the road. Within fifteen minutes, they were in the Clausell area. Before they could park, Cashmere, Sam, Malinda, and Geronimo ran out.

Each one brought their overnight bag in. Cashmere had prepared a delicious meal. She had baked salmon, sautéed spinach, and rice pilaf. Malinda baked a pineapple upside down cake. Sam made the peach tea. Geronimo brought a container of vanilla ice cream. What a feast that was for all of them.

While they were eating, Sam said, "Look what I gave Malinda." It was another engagement ring. It was nice.

Jasmine asked, "Is that a diamond?"

"Yes, it is. It's almost two carats." Sam responded.

"Good gracious big brother, I know that may have cost you a pretty penny."

"Under normal circumstances it might have cost more; but Malinda and I did some freelance work for a jeweler in Birmingham. He was so pleased with our work that he gave us a pretty good deal on the rings, so much so, that we felt like it was almost free. In fact, this was our motivation for having a small wedding where we could use the money we have for housing."

"Mom, I don't believe I have ever seen any engagement ring that big before." Jasmine stated.

"Momma hasn't either," Cashmere mentioned.

Skyler was extremely quiet. Not one acknowledgement that the ring was big, beautiful, or captivating. No congratulations shared. He was deep in thought because he had not considered the idea of giving Jasmine a ring until now. He wondered where he would get the money. Unnecessarily, he felt a lot of pressure since he had regularly spoken about marriage. This gigantic ring on this petite girl's finger totally consumed Skyler. He noticed how all at the table paid attention to the ring as the buzz concerning the ring took over the room. Even Geronimo was impressed. Sam had surprised everyone there, except Malinda. The irony of this shocker was that they all were there to express their interest in marriage, while getting their specific questions answered.

River did not feel the pressure since he had recently met Lillie. They were delighted and contributed to the buzz at the dining room table. River fittingly said, "Congratulations! Man, when I grow up, I want to be like you."

"Son you have done well." Geronimo clapped.

Overjoyed, Cashmere spoke. "Sam that is wonderful. Malinda, you are one special woman."

Lillie asked, "Is this what I can look forward too when I get engaged?"

"Congratulations Sam & Malinda. I am so happy for you. I think your ring is beautiful. I don't know if I would want a ring when I get married." Jasmine confessed.

Skyler was last to express his view of the ring. "Sam the ring is very nice. I hope you and Malinda have a great engagement and subsequent great wedding." In the recesses of his brain, he was trying to remember if Jasmine said she did not think she wanted a ring. He could not wait until later to confirm her statement, so he asked, "Jasmine did you say you are not sure if you want a ring when you get married?"

"Yes. That's correct."

"Most women really want a diamond engagement ring. Why do you feel that way?"

"Actually Skyler, I never thought too much about getting married; therefore, naturally I wouldn't be dreaming about an engagement ring. But for me, it seems like I would prefer having a wedding more so than a diamond ring. What about you. Do you want to have a wedding ring?"

"Well Jasmine, I have always dreamed of getting married, but I never thought about the ring until tonight."

Lillie decided to add her two cents to the conversation. "Well, I want it all. The courtship. The ring. The bridal parties. The wedding. The reception. The honeymoon. Then I want the house. The housewarming parties. The baby. The baby showers. Oh yes the husband." Everyone laughed so hard.

River remarked, "Do yawl see that I have an expensive girl to take care of. I got to get a job."

Lillie added, "I cain't say it's solely young women like me and Malinda who want a big ring. Looks like Coach Van Damme has a wife that wants it all too. Jasmine did you see that big ring she had on her finger?"

Jasmine asked, "Lillie, how did you see all of that? You were not talking to her. I was talking to her."

Lillie responded, "While you were talking, I was looking."

Cashmere asked, "When did you see Coach Van Damme's wife?"

Jasmine replied, "When we stopped at Walmart to take a bathroom break. Coach Van Damme was with her too. As a matter of fact, she asked how daddy was doing?" Geronimo lowered his head.

"I told her that my daddy is doing fine. My

momma is doing fine too. Then we left. Malinda and Sam, you two gave us a lot to think about when it comes to rings. It's really interesting that neither Skyler nor I had talked about having an engagement ring."

Geronimo decided to speak up, as well as take the lead in organizing the rest of the evening. "Well kids you all must be tired. Let's finish up dinner and get you home so you can rest. The girls are going to stay with Cashmere. The boys are going with me. We can have a light breakfast at Cashmere's house tomorrow morning. Then we will have two car groups to take a tour of Monroeville. Cashmere and I decided to have a cookout in the backyard at her Spa. The girls will get beauty treatments. The boys will play billiards. By then, we should have bonded a little more. Does that sound good?"

They all accepted that it would be good. They finished dinner and cleaned up the kitchen. The boys gathered their bags to leave with Geronimo when

Cashmere approached them. She told Geronimo she was so happy that he took the lead in organizing everything because she had a long day at work. Then she gave him a hug.

Chapter 22

Everyone was up early at Geronimo's house, excited to eat breakfast at Cashmere's house. They were having a little man talk when Cashmere called Geronimo and told him that breakfast would be ready in ten minutes. They only lived about three miles apart. They jumped in the car and was there in no time. As the girls were finishing preparing the meal of French toast, scrambled eggs and bacon, the boys helped themselves to a fruit salad made with apples, blueberries, raspberries, and bananas. Cashmere glanced at Geronimo and asked if he would like to say a prayer. Sam and Jasmine looked at each other. Their look showed that something might be there, even after five years divorced.

Geronimo said the quickest prayer. "Thank you God for this food." They began eating. It felt like home for everyone. They all pitched in to clean the kitchen. They headed out for their tour. Since Cashmere and Geronimo lived in Clausell, they went to the Clausell Community Center first, where there were a host of things to do. The Park was situated on about forty or fifty acres. There was a swimming pool, three tennis courts, three softball fields, a pavilion, a playground, and four basketball half-courts. When Cashmere's momma was a little girl, the swimming pool was the only thing that was there on the forty acres.

Next, they went to the Old Monroe County Courthouse located near the Heritage Museum. This grabbed a lot of attention worldwide because this courthouse was associated with writer, Harper Lee, the author of *To Kill a Mockingbird.* The last attraction they went to see was the Bronze Sculpture trail.

Shortly after that, they went to Cashmere's Spa for the cookout.

Geronimo fired up the grill. Cashmere had already prepared chicken to go on the grill, along with hotdogs and hamburgers. It was a nice fall day. Some of the trees had changed colors to a brownish orange, to red and to yellow. They finished with the cook-out about four o'clock in the evening. Cashmere gave everyone a tour of her salon, then rushed the guys out. It was time for some real girl talk. They agreed to meet back up about eight o' clock in the evening at the spa.

Cashmere had two estheticians and two massage therapists come in for one hour. The girls went through the wet area which included the sauna and steam room before their service was to begin at six p.m.

Lillie wanted to get the facial. Jasmine wanted to get the massage. Malinda wanted to get the facial. Cashmere wanted to get the massage. The schedule worked out beautifully. When they all finished their service, it was about seven p.m. Then they went to *The Relaxation Zone* room upstairs.

Cashmere gave each one some strawberry cucumber infused water. It was so refreshing.

She asked, "How do you girls feel being pampered today?" Each was so thankful.

Jasmine said, "Momma I want to get right into my question because an hour will pass in no time. "Why did you and daddy want to get married?"

"Jasmine, the fundamental reason people get married is because they love each other. They want an environment where they can receive emotional support and give emotional support. In other words, they want to have companionship. When a person gets married, they should have an environment where each spouse feels loved, secure, appreciated, and needed in a very special way. So, that is why we got married."

"So, momma what if one of the marriage mates

does not keep his or her end of the promise?"

"It may cause a person to look for love in all the wrong places. Darling, marriage mates should become one flesh. If that does not happen, this may cause the other spouse to feel deprived emotionally which may cause self-esteem challenges. It does not start out like wanting sexual gratification. It comes later after the spouse has received emotional support from someone other than the spouse. The person feels entirely comfortable."

Malinda asked, "How can I keep that from happening Ms. Summers?"

"The first thing you must do is become a good listener. Now, if you can do that, it makes the other person feel really special. Besides that, you must protect your relationship from scallywags."

"What is a scallywag?" Malinda asked.

"It's a Southern term for a traitor. You see, a person may try to be your friend with a view to seducing your husband. Now, that is simply a word of caution because not all women are like that. Learn to have open honest communication with your spouse. Your spouse should not feel that if he tells you something that might make you upset, it may cause you to leave, to simply walk away from the marriage. Each person needs to feel secure girls. Never allow your spouse to emotionally unload on someone else what should be for you. Communicate with your spouse like you are best friends, like I think you all are doing."

"Momma, did you ever see a scallywag?"

"Honey, there were scallywags all around. I tried to do the best I could to protect my marriage."

"Momma, after five years divorced, what do you think you and daddy could have done differently?"

"Grow up. We had a fairytale view of marriage. But when we got pregnant with Sam, I guess my anger flared up because I felt your dad was insensitive to me in every way imaginable. He would say things like you are totally emotional. Then I would start crying. He would say it again. Little did he know, that was the wrong thing to tell me.

"I was an overwhelmed nineteen-year-old. Still, I am a thirty-nine-year-old with emotional needs. Women are plain different from men. Men want to solve problems. We just want someone to listen because we in many cases know how to solve the problem. Consequently, a husband would need to know that making his wife feel precious, as well as capable, builds her up rather than speaking condescendingly, which would chip away at her self-worth."

"Ms. Summers what are good things to talk about with your husband?"

"Talk about everything. Talk about everyday things with each other Malinda. For example: What happened at work? What happened at the supermarket? What happened with the neighbor's dog? What his momma said when she called. What you told her when she called.

They all laughed as Cashmere continued. "Remember to treat him like you are best friends. In Psychology Today, I read that men's lack of responsiveness to their wives' emotional needs is both a cause and an effect of unhappiness in many marriages."

"Ms. Summers, what if you don't want to talk about the problems?"

"Lillie if you suppress your feelings, it could destroy your body. Once a person internalizes something, it eats at you. You may start to have unresolved health problems. Perhaps, you may have headaches that will not go away or stomach problems that do not get better.

"Girls this is very important. Do not commit adultery. That is when you have sex with someone other than your marriage mate. It breaks up families. Some people never recover. It breaks up friendships too."

"So, momma is that what happened with you and

daddy?"

"Your daddy did not commit adultery. Neither did I commit adultery."

"Well momma, Why did you divorce?"

"Girls the primary reason was lack of communication. We did not know how to talk with each other. Jasmine your daddy has grown a lot. So, have I. We now have two beautiful children that are doing what we should have done. Seek out the advice of older long-time married couples that would help you, tell you the truth. Although, your daddy and I do not totally fit what I just said, what enables us to comment on the subject is that we have learned a lot from our mistakes. That means also we could have eliminated a lot of heartache if we had asked more questions."

"Did you and daddy spend a lot of time together? I remember that you worked a lot."

"Your dad and I worked a lot. No, we did not spend time together. We should have. I think each of us built up resentment because we did a lot of things separate. If we had shared the responsibilities, it would not have felt so burdensome. Here I am a teenager, one year married, at nineteen years old, having a baby. That was not the life I saw for myself.

"So as much as you can, stick with your spouse, which is a protection for the both of you. Be each other's bodyguard. Each other's protector. If you find yourself letting insignificant things get in the way of spending time together, there is a possibility that there is a weak link in your marriage. Identify the weak link and jump on that weakness to strengthen it. If not, that could lead to unnecessary temptations, further problems which could end your marriage."

Cashmere asked the two young athletes a question. "Jasmine. Lillie. If your experienced Coach saw that you had a simple thing to work on such as putting your hands up when you were guarding someone, what benefit would that have on your game?"

Jasmine answered, "The benefit of doing that

consistently helps with my defense and so the offensive team is not easily able to pass the ball throughout the lanes, which ultimately keeps them from scoring. And in addition to that, I could hinder the passing and retrieve the ball and score."

"Jasmine that's what it means when you work on a simple problem in your marriage before it becomes serious. You beef up your defense program that would involve patching up the weak link, be it effective communication, time spent together or cherishing your mate."

"Ms. Summers, I know that I am not very athletic but that makes perfect sense to me. Handle the problem before it gets bigger."

"Yes, that is correct Malinda."

"Momma, one final question. Is it important that I get an engagement ring?"

"Honey if you don't remember anything else, please remember this, a ring doesn't make the marriage."

"I got it momma. Thank you."

Malinda commented, "I got it too Ms. Summers."

Lillie commented, "I got it too Ms. Summers. A ring doesn't make the marriage at all; but I want to get one."

"Lillie, I am not against engagement rings. It is a beautiful gift that your future husband gives you as a promise to love you, to marry you, to spend the rest of his life with you. In his mind, it is a contract. He wants you to know that he is planning on staying with you. And when you accept it, it becomes a binding agreement or contract. I hope that does not sound too technical. That is the best way I can explain it."

"Ms. Summers. I really do get it. Some women are so excited about the ring that they do not consider all what is involved with marriage. For some women, the ring is a show piece. For some women, it alerts others that you are getting married or that you are married. Then again, some guys do not respect the ring if you tell them you are engaged. So that is why I see and understand what you mean when you said that a ring does not make the marriage. Thank you for explaining that more because I want to be the one who has a proper motive in accepting an engagement ring."

"You made some good points Lillie. I believe that you understand. I did not want you to think that I was against having an engagement ring. This conversation was about focusing on the more important things of a marriage. How to work at having a successful marriage. We all love to receive gifts. We like to give gifts. We appreciate when our loved ones give us a gift as a token of their love for us."

Jasmine said, "I have a question that is a little off the subject, but I want to know if Malinda and Lillie have hope chests?"

Malinda said, "Yes, I have one. I have almost filled it up. I started putting items in my hope chest at twelve years old."

"Why did you start so early?" Jasmine wondered.

"Remember Jasmine. Originally, I was going to get married at eighteen years old."

"Sorry Malinda. I do not know how I forgot that. It seems so long ago that I learned about that."

Lillie replied, "Yes, I have a hope chest, but I left it in South Carolina. When I go home, I got to put other things in there for marriage. I just had a lot of basketball memorabilia in there. That was what I thought about then."

Jasmine said, "I have one that momma made for me when I was fifteen years old. It is beautiful. So I will start putting items in there that would be special for me whenever I get married."

Finally, Cashmere said, "I have a hope chest too. I have one that my daughter gave me at a surprise party. I don't have to add anything else to it."

Malinda and Lillie were so impressed that Jasmine saw the need to help her momma have a new start. They hugged her because it was such a thoughtful gesture. Cashmere joined in by sharing briefly with the girls how Jasmine's support was one of the most impactful expressions of love that she had received in a long time.

Cashmere continued, "Any more questions girls? This session was for you. I hope this has helped you. I know that it has helped me. I really would like to hear what Geronimo told the boys. I can see that he has changed, and I am happy for him, just as I have changed, and I hope he is happy for me. However, it would be quite interesting to hear his take on what he has learned."

While the girls were having their spa services performed, Geronimo got right into the discussion as soon as he entered the billiard room.

"Hey guys, when Cashmere asked me about hosting a sleep over for yawl, I was so excited. When she told me what you all wanted to talk about, I was a little skeptical because my marriage had not been totally successful. But, after thinking about it a little more, I realized that I had a lot of things to share. If I could communicate what worked and what did not work, it would be of value not only to you but to me. To have my son, my daughter's boyfriend, the family cousin, and me altogether was an opportunity that I had to take. Let me ask you a question. Are you all good at billiards?"

Sam said, "Daddy you know that I'm good because you taught me. A little rusty, but good."

Skyler said, "Mr. Summers, I'm pretty good at it. Let's say I play the game really good."

"River, what about you?"

"Well cousin Geronimo, I prefer dancing rather than playing billiards. But I will say, I can play a little."

"Okay, you guys have enough experience to play me. Sam you make the toss."

Sam asked his dad if he wanted heads or tails. Of course, Geronimo wanted the head of the coin. Sam walked between all the guys allowing each one to stand around him in a circle. He threw a quarter, high into the air. As the coin dropped quickly, it rolled then laid on the side. Sam ran up to the coin with his hands spread so no one would pick it up. They all bent over to see the coin except Geronimo. Sam stood with the coin in his hand and said, "Dad you won the toss."

"Thanks son. Young men, I am so happy we can play billiards together. One reason is that you have made it clear that you are interested in girls. I mean girls because women require a deeper education. The second reason is I'm going to beat you good, so you know what it feels like to lose. I won the toss, so I will break. While I'm winning this game, I will tell you the truth about marriage.

"Billiards or the game of pool require good foot work to place the pool shot where you want the ball to go. You must keep finger and eye contact control. Lastly, choosing the right move at the right time is the key to winning.

"Although I wanted to get married, my footwork

was missing. I had challenges, left and right, when I was younger. I had no self-control. I could not discipline my body parts. I could not decide what to do first. Hence, I lost the only woman that I really loved. Do you all have self-control?"

"Daddy, I believe that I have self-control."

Skyler said, "Mr. Summers, I have self-control. I am an athlete. That is necessary to becoming a well-rounded athlete."

River said, "I have self-control sometimes."

"Ok Gentlemen. I understand what you are trying to say. The self-control I am talking about has to do with something that you have little experience in, women. However, after you take this beating tonight, choose for yourselves. Do you want to become a loser, or do you want to become a winner?

"A major part in courting a girl is knowing everything about her background, her parents, her likes, her dislikes and her goals. When you play pool, you must be very familiar with the fabric of the table surface. It will tell you the speed of the balls and the impact of the angles. Very important to winning. Like marriage, the game of billiards will continue the way you start it. If you score on the break as I did, you can set the tempo of the game and run the table. If you do not, someone else will. Your chances of losing just tripled, purely, like I am doing to you tonight.

"In marriage, if you start it right by noticing the surface of the family, the person that you are interested in, remember this, 'the apple doesn't fall far from the tree.' You can make your moves according to knowledge, and not be swinging at the air. The mistake I made was not peaking at the right time. What I mean by this is, as a man, I should have known that girls turn into women. About every seven to ten years, their values change.

"The activities we did while we were under twenty-five were much more expensive, much more time consuming than over twenty-five. She needs tenderness for sure under twenty-five; but it will increase tremendously each decade. Even more so, the emotional pressure, the social pressure of what a woman wants, increases as she gets older.

"As a White man Skyler, will you be able to deal with the pressures of a Black woman. It's like the pressure of scoring the eight ball when there are no more balls on the table. In the South, the pressure to not scratch the eight ball is scary because you will lose the game if you scratch and hit the eight ball in a hole that you did not call out.

"Young men, to win in marriage, you must prepare well. A good start is to master your footwork. Cultivate self-control by knowing everything you can about your potential marriage mate. Choose the right moves in your courtship. What do I mean by that?"

"Daddy, I believe that you mean not rush into marriage. Plan everything."

"Cousin Geronimo, I have good moves. I know what I want. No one has to push me to go after it."

"I think the move I made is when I wanted to speak with you and Ms. Summers. Late last night I started thinking about the money associated with purchasing an engagement ring. Certainly, I want the best for my future wife, and I hope she wants the same for me." Skyler emphasized.

Geronimo dignified them. "I see you all have opinions. And that is good. So, let me make it clearer. Number one, can you financially afford a wife? Number two, do you have clean family building habits? Number three, do you know your fiancé and her family well? Number four, do you love her sweat? Number five, are you willing to protect your wife each decade of her life she is married to you, no matter what happens?"

Concluding the game, Geronimo calls out, "Eight ball, side pocket, after it kisses off the center diamond." The eyes of the three young men traveled to the side pocket where Geronimo directed the ball. He made the shot. An angry outburst occurred!

River yelled, "Do you believe he made that shot? Crazy cuz. Crazy!"

Geronimo stood up from the shot, placed his pool stick in the rack and whispered, "Game is over. All the balls are off the table. I am sorry I had to beat you all so bad. You know we could be here all night, but we cain't be late for the second part of our evening. It is going to take about fifteen minutes to get back to Cashmere's spa by eight p.m. Let's hit it."

Skyler sighed. "Can you believe he scored all of those balls and won the game? We did not even get a chance to touch the table. Unreal."

They made it back to the Spa about three minutes early. Flabbergasted by their promptness, Cashmere said, "I felt that you all would get carried away playing billiards. But I am certainly impressed that you made it back safely and on time. Did you all talk, or did you all just play billiards?"

Geronimo answered, "I have changed a lot my

dear. I respect your time and others, a little different than from before. To answer your question, we did both. Surprised? Right."

"Mom, dad gave us some good pointers."

"Sam, please let your momma know if there were lessons you learned that you could share with us?"

"Plenty momma. I want to share with Malinda first."

"Ok. I'm amazed again son."

Geronimo asked, "What about your evening? Was it fun for you all?"

All the girls answered. "It was a lot of fun. We learned a lot."

Jasmine said, "Daddy I asked questions about you all. I got some very good insight. But what I want to share with everyone here is that I am so proud of momma. She has built a successful business. She has taken time to help me and Sam by hosting our friends. Thank you too daddy. I am very happy right now. I am thankful that Skyler came up with the idea. My massage was great. So far, the trip has been truly successful. I wondered how you, momma, and daddy, would work together while under this setting. It has been magnificent. It is nothing more beautiful for us, than to see both of our parents getting along well, even though you are not married now. I love you both so much!"

Geronimo's eyes welled up with water. Cashmere went over to hug Jasmine then Sam. "Remember we still want the best for our children. Your daddy and I will do our best to make that happen."

River said, "Okay that's great. What are we going to do the rest of the evening?"

Cashmere answered his question. "We have something that would bring you enjoyment. We have a slide show of the children growing up. We have a few slides of you too River. So, we will head back to my house for some snacks and a slide show. After the slide show, we have another surprise that we all can appreciate.

"For all of us? What is it Cousin Cashmere?"

"I think I said a surprise."

This was a spectacular day for Jasmine and Sam. Skyler had the right idea. He recognized that he must understand Jasmine's parents, seek their advice, and apply it. His mother would provide a complete picture for him.

Chapter 23

The slideshow was hilarious. Not only did they have photos of the children. Geronimo, Cashmere, and River were in some of the photos. The doorbell rang. Jasmine went to the door. She was so surprised to see Marylou.

"Marylou you made it. I asked momma to invite you. Is Tommy with you?"

"No, he couldn't make it. He is out of town."

"You remember Skyler?"

"How could I ever forget him? Hey Skyler. How are you doing?"

"Doing good Marylou and you?"

"Doing good. How is my cousin River?

"Marylou I'm doing good. You look really good."

"Thanks River. So, do you. Hey Mr. Summers, Ms. Summers."

"Marylou, this is Lillie Gray, my roommate and River's girlfriend."

"Good to meet you Lillie. You are pretty tall there. So, do you like to dance?"

"How did you know?" Lillie inquired.

"Because I learned the hard way how much River likes to dance. I am sure yawl will hit it off well. Did I make it in time for the surprise?"

Cashmere responded, "Yes you did. Let's move the furniture a little way back. Ok Sam. You can start."

"Tonight, we have a little competition scheduled. Here are the rules. You can have a partner, or you can participate without one. It is a dance contest. Only one dance act at a time. We have four song selections in this hat. The one song that we select from the hat will be the choice everyone will have to dance to. You must complete the entire song. The act that gets the biggest applause will get a fifty-dollar gift card from Walmart. Are you ready? Any questions? Daddy will you select a song from the hat. Ok here it is. *2 Legit 2 Quit* by M.C. Hammer."

In the background was a video playing with Hammer dancing. First up was Skyler and Jasmine. They were pretty good, but the music was a little fast for them. Next was Sam and Malinda. They danced ok, but not to exciting. River and Lillie were next. They tore the living room up with their soulful dance moves. Then Cashmere and Geronimo got up. Surprisingly, not only did they dance, they sang the lyrics.

Then someone said, "Marylou I can dance with you so you can have a partner."

"No, I will be fine by myself. I have a song that I like. I brought it with me. So, I know this will disqualify me to get the prize, but here it is. It's *Fine* by Mary J Blige. I have been trying to be more open, so I have been practicing how to dance."

River was totally shocked. Marylou had changed from leaving an auditorium when he was dancing at a talent show, to dancing in front of an audience that knew she did not and could not dance. Encouraged by her moxie or her courage and spirit, everyone jumped on the dance floor to support her. That was the most fun Marylou had ever experienced in her life.

Yes, the prize went to River and Lillie. They wanted to honor Marylou with the prize because it took courage for her to dance. Little did they know that Marylou started taking dance lessons about a year ago. In any case, it was a fun evening.

After everyone settled down, Geronimo said, "We got to go. I have had a very long day. I need to sleep."

The others agreed. So, Geronimo took his crew over to his apartment. Jasmine asked Marylou to stay over with the other girls at Cashmere's house. She did. It was a wonderful day.

Chapter 24

Sunday morning had come quickly. Cashmere called Geronimo to see if everyone had gotten up. They had. So, she told them to come for breakfast. She and the girls had made breakfast burritos. They had not expected that Cashmere was planning on going to a spiritual service.

Instead of sending the guys back to get a little more dressed up, she said, "Ok, this is where we go to get spiritual refreshment. Don't have time to change clothes. Let's go. It's only an hour." The boys, as well as Geronimo went with Cashmere and the girls.

Only about seventy-five people could comfortably fit in this small building. However, they all could not believe that the subject was on marriage. Cashmere and Geronimo had never heard anything like what this speaker said. He said that the only scriptural grounds for divorce before God was adultery, whether committed by either marriage mate. Additionally, if anyone divorced because of something like irreconcilable differences, or I am tired of you, or I do not love you anymore or I found somebody else, does not give them the freedom to remarry. If the person remarried, God considered the person an adulterer.

It was a new concept that made Cashmere and Geronimo think. After the service, Geronimo asked Cashmere, "Did you ever think that we were still married in God's sight?"

"Certainly not! Never heard anything like that before. I was startled by the statement; but I will do some research."

"Where will you begin with your research?" Geronimo asked.

"There is an older couple that is probably in their

early seventies that live down the street from me. That couple has been living there for about two years. I have talked to the wife before. She made some good points on how bad things were in the world; but I had a lot of stuff on my mind and was too busy to talk. I think I'll ask her because she told me she and her husband study the scriptures all the time."

"Well, let me know what you find out."

"I will. You know that entire hour went over all of our guests' head. I believe they were super tired. All I saw was their heads rolling around and up and down. River asked me what were we all doing later. He looked so tired."

"Cashmere let's go to your Spa to relax. I know I would enjoy that. The guys might appreciate that too. I know the girls would. What do you think?"

"I think that is an excellent idea Geronimo."

When Cashmere asked the youngsters if they wanted to go to the Spa to relax for a couple of hours, they all said yes. By then, it would be time for them to get back to Tuscaloosa.

Cashmere said, “We can get take-out from the Dairy Queen.” So, they got hamburgers, french-fries, and milk shakes. After everyone finished eating, they all went up to *The Relaxation Zone* room where the soft music and refreshing waterfall brought a calmness like when one was on the beach.

Cashmere had a couple of older lounges downstairs that Geronimo brought upstairs so everyone would have their own lounge. They all got a chance to rest. After resting for about ninety minutes, Geronimo reminded them that they needed to get back to the house to pack, so that they could get back on the road.

When they finished packing, they got into the car and left for Tuscaloosa. River was so happy that they had rested, especially since he had to drive back. Although it was a short trip of about two and a half hours from Tuscaloosa to Monroeville, it was worth the sacrifice because each of them felt closer to Mr. and Ms. Summers and to each other.

They arrived on campus about seven o' clock in the evening. They did not waste anytime chatting. Each one went to his or her dorm room. Jasmine and Lillie took a shower and went right to sleep.

Monday morning was a little easier on them after the long night sleep. Each couple had received valuable information from Cashmere and Geronimo. Now it was back to school with a more comprehensive idea of what marriage was all about. They appeared to be content with what they learned.

Within a couple of months, Sam and Malinda would be getting married and making a new life for themselves. In the meantime, Cashmere visited her neighbor who was happy for the visit. She told her neighbor what had happened at the service.

Cashmere wanted to know if what she learned was true about what constituted a divorce in God's eyes. The woman was very familiar with the explanation given at the service. She shared the scriptures on the subject that she had learned from a child. Cashmere asked, "How do you know all of this?"

The neighbor answered, "I made it a goal to spend some time studying the Bible every day since I was a young girl, just like my parents taught me to do. My parents said that you have a schedule for school, just add a few minutes more every day to read the Holy Book." The neighbor precisely answered her question and told her if she had any other questions, feel free to stop by again.

Cashmere called Geronimo and asked if he could meet her at the convenient mart. She told him everything that she learned from her neighbor.

Geronimo asked, "Why did you want to find that out? Do you still love me?"

"Yes, I do Geronimo. You are the father of our two children."

"No, I mean like when you first met me and there were no children."

Cashmere blushed. She said, "I prayed not to love you anymore."

"What happened?"

"God did not answer my prayer."

"Does that mean you still love me?"

"I guess so."

"I'm so glad to hear that Cashmere. You are the only woman that I have ever loved. I cried like a baby when I saw Coach Van Damme touch your hand. I wanted to hurt him; but you no longer belonged to me. It was tough. While we were married, I did the best I could under the circumstances. Now that I have grown a little wiser and I have made changes, I would like the opportunity to court you again. I would like to take advantage of the advice I gave the young men this weekend. Can we try again please? I promise I will love you better than I did before."

"How would that happen Geronimo? What if it didn't work out again?"

"Skyler wanted to know what the best way was to court Jasmine. I told him to be positive was the first thing to do. I am going to be positive about us. We know what our mistakes were. We can date quietly to see if you are ok with it. No pressure. I promise. Indeed, we had a wonderful time this weekend. You are the best dance partner I have ever had. Two good friends getting re-acquainted. Can we try?"

"Yes. Let's not tell the children right away Geronimo. We would not want them to hope for something that might not happen. Let's completely be real about that."

"I agree Cashmere. If after a few weeks, it does not seem right, we can go back to the way things are now. Being friendly because of the kids. I really am attracted to how you have matured so much since our separation."

Geronimo kissed Cashmere on the cheek.

"Let's talk tomorrow."

They got in their cars and drove off. Cashmere felt like she was in high school again. She pulled into her driveway, glanced up to look at herself in the rear-view mirror, touched her cheek and thought, "I'm not interested in any other man in Monroeville. Is this right? Can it work?"

Once she got inside, she went straight to the bedroom to take her shower. Usually, she waited up for Sam to come home before she went to bed. Tonight, she did not wait on Sam to come home. She turned out the light, went to bed with thoughts of Geronimo on her mind.

Sure enough, the next morning Geronimo called. They chatted briefly. He asked, "How do you feel today about what we discussed last night?"

"I feel the same as last night. I am ok with us dating. Please know that I don't want our kids to know right away."

"That is ok for me too Cashmere."

When Cashmere arrived at her Spa, she checked the spa out as she regularly did after each weekend. This time it was a tad bit different because she thought seriously about how it would be to start dating her ex-husband. Would she have to change her life again after five years making her own decisions? Would she have to share her business with her ex-husband who may not be a good businessperson? Would he slip back into the behavior he had prior to the divorce? Would remarrying him make her look needy?

On the other hand, she reasoned that they both had clearly changed. They both loved each other, and the children, which at one time had put a major strain on their marriage were now adults preparing to get married. Would they have a new set of challenges with adult children? Cashmere figured that it could be that they would not face the earlier challenges. She was mildly excited, but highly skeptical. Then she said to herself, "Be positive."

Cashmere recalled how Jasmine had commended her openly to all about how proud she was of her momma's accomplishments. So, Cashmere took pride in her daughter's statements which brought her back to a positive outlook. Genuinely torn by their decision to date within minutes after they talked, she called Geronimo.

"Geronimo I'm having a melt-down. Honestly, I have become afraid. Are you having second thoughts?"

"Do not let your heart be troubled. Exercise faith. Not at all Cashmere. I am having beautiful thoughts about you, about the opportunity to make things up to you, about the way I would care for you. In what way I would make your dreams, my dreams. My thoughts are good. I am not afraid of life anymore. I want to take pleasure in life. I am overjoyed that I have a second opportunity to live it with the woman that I love. The woman who has not become angry because of how her life was but remembering how her life is. I am thinking how I can make you feel like you are my queen. And if that is not enough, I can get on bended knee, ask you to marry me today so that I can make up for lost time.

"I don't mean to scare you because all I have

dreamed about is loving you and caring for you. Having a home with you is paramount. Building a home with you is supreme. Because the way I am living is not what I want. I have a house, but not a home. I know my mistakes. I have always wanted a second chance. This weekend made my desire clear. My conversation with the young men heightened my courage to ask you for another chance. My love was sure, but my courage needed a pick me up. That was the only thing that I was missing to approach you. What more can I do to show my sincerity? I will do it. Hold on a second Cashmere. Do you remember this song?"

He played this song by Luther Vandross, "A House is Not a Home." While that song was playing, Cashmere's tears rolled down her cheek, the cheek that Gerónimo kissed the night before. Music spoke to her heart. And out of all the words Geronimo said, this song made her respond.

She said, "Yes. We can try. If we decide to

remarry, I think we should get marriage counseling this time."

"I agree. You know Cashmere, our marriage changed a lot when Sam was born. It changed again when Jasmine was born. The irony is that the children wanted us to help them out with what to expect when they got married. It appears that it is going to help us also. I would like to ask you a question."

"What is it Geronimo?"

"Will you forgive me for the heartache that I caused you?"

"Ahhh, Geronimo. I did not expect this. Thanks." She fanned her face with her hand, trying not to overreact by jumping up and grabbing him. But she couldn't anyway because he was on the telephone. She had waited for such a long time to hear his plea for forgiveness and to forgive him, when she said, "Yes, I forgive you. And I would like to ask you a question?"

"Ok. I hope I can answer it."

"Will you forgive me for the heartache that I caused you?"

"What heartache? You were doing what you were supposed to do and more. I was the slacker. You looked to me for strength and support. I could not provide that. But so that we would be on an even playing field, of course, I forgive you. So, we are two good forgivers. We did not know how to forgive or let hurt feelings go when we were younger. Thank you for giving me another chance. So, when are you available for our first date?"

"Cashmere giggled. "I think we already had it."

"I guess you are right. I would like to make dinner for you. When are you available?"

"I'm finished with work by six o'clock. Any day this week will be good. But I would prefer to go to a public place."

"That's good Cashmere. I should have asked you what you would like to do. Well, where would you like to go?

"I have not had pizza in a long time. That would be a nice splurge for me. Would that be okay for you Geronimo?"

"Come to think of it. I have not eaten pizza in a long time either. I might even have some wings with my pizza."

"Oh Geronimo. That will really be nice. I could meet you there about seven tomorrow night. I genuinely would like to keep our courtship really honorable. I would like to refrain from sexual intercourse until we are married. I hope that does not sound weird."

"No Cashmere, it sounds chaste. If our courtship is honorable that is the foundation of having an honorable marriage. I like it. It is even more intriguing. Well, I agree with the rules. From my standpoint, I know you have built a successful business. I am proud of you. But I want to take care of you financially.

"I would like you to use your money for your

business in whatever way you want or help the children if they need it in addition to what I will do for them. I certainly feel that it is my responsibility to take care of you and our children. I hope you feel that my wish is honorable and not that I am belittling you or your accomplishments. As a Black man, I want to make sure that I'm known as a provider."

"Geronimo that is really commendable. Thank you for saying what you are thinking about. This conversation is making me feel really good. I feel so much better. So, I gotta go. I will see you tomorrow evening."

Cashmere was ecstatic about the possibility of rebuilding a marriage that never had a strong foundation. Positive thoughts reinvigorated her.

Chapter 25

Malinda and Sam would begin their employment in January 2020 with the same Advertising Company. Almost one month before their start date, each of them received a letter from their new employer, saying that effective immediately, the company was on a hiring freeze and all offers were on hold until further notice. Malinda had finished reading her letter when Sam was calling to inform her that he had just received the same letter. They decided to meet at a nearby coffee shop to discuss what they would do now.

Earlier they had decided to have their wedding during the holidays, so that they could begin their new jobs shortly after the wedding. Now that the job situation had changed, they had a decision to make, and besides that, they had a little more latitude and less pressure to have the wedding during the holidays.

Although neither wanted a big wedding, without a job offer, they decided to postpone the wedding until late spring. Actually, what they learned from Geronimo and Cashmere helped them to see that they didn't need to rush to get married without a job. When Cashmere got home from work on Tuesday, she found Sam at home. He had prepared dinner for her. Surprised that he was in the kitchen preparing dinner, Cashmere asked, "What's going on Sam?"

"What do you mean momma?"

"Dinner for me? It looks pretty elaborate."

"Yes. I was compelled to make dinner for you tonight before I shared the news that I received today."

"What is it?"

"The company that was going to hire Malinda and me, sent each of us a letter stating that the company was on a hiring freeze and that our jobs were no longer available."

"So, what did you and Malinda decide to do?"

"We decided to postpone our wedding until late May. Also, we talked about what we learned from you all; therefore, we want to wait to get a good paying job before we get married. That means I would need to stay with you a little longer to save the little money I'm making now, along with trying to find better employment. Will that be all right?"

"Now I get it. That's why you made this fabulous meal. Son that's fine. Always count the cost. By all means, you can stay to save your money. Did you change your mind about only the two of you would be in the wedding party?"

"No momma. We did not change our mind about that. It will still be simple."

"That's very good. Well, I might be able to give you a few hours a week at the Spa if you need it."

"Thanks momma. I'll let you know. I still have

some options locally. I was hoping for that job because it was in our field. But we can use the time to prepare even more for the wedding."

"Oh, by the way Sam, I have a dinner appointment tomorrow evening with a friend. I'll be home around nine p.m."

"Ok momma. That's fine."

"I'm going to get a shower and head to bed. I am a little tired. Goodnight."

The next day Cashmere woke up with a wheezy stomach; probably because she did not eat dinner the night before. She prepared an English muffin with peanut butter and a cup of ginger tea. That seemed to make her feel better. She had a full day with no major problems. She was not sure if she were excited to go on a date with Geronimo or if she were excited about the pizza. She smiled when she realized that the pizza was at the top of her thoughts.

She only had a small salad with a few chunks of tuna for lunch, expecting that she would get a couple of slices of her favorite pizza at dinner. When she finished work, she decided to head over to the Pizza Hut, as she got there about ten minutes before Geronimo arrived. When Geronimo came, he was so surprised to see Cashmere already there. He greeted her with his smiling eyes and gave her a single pink rose tied with a long curly pink ribbon. And after accepting the rose, she gave him a half hug as she patted him on the back. She reciprocated with the same twinkle in her eyes, while saying, "Thank you for the beautiful rose. I have been looking forward to this all day long."

"Me too. I was thinking about you all day long." Geronimo echoed.

"Cashmere mumbled, "I had a couple of things on my mine."

"Is it anything serious Cashmere?"

"Yes, really serious Geronimo."

"Would you like to share it with me? What can I do?"

"I have been thinking about my favorite pizza all day long and contemplating if I should try another kind of pizza. So, you can help me by ordering the pizza!"

"What a blow to my self-esteem Cashmere."

"My goodness. You came in at a close second."

"I know a hungry lady when I see one."

Geronimo ordered a large thick crust pepperoni pizza with sausage, mushrooms, bell peppers, onions, and extra cheese. They both ordered lemonade. As they were waiting on their order, Cashmere asked Geronimo if he had a good day. He responded, "Relatively good. What about you?"

"I had a good day."

"When was the last time you had a bad day Cashmere?"

"Well, I'll have to go back a few years?"

"A few years?"

"Yeah. I had the worse day when I was leaving work. I said hello to you. You walked right by me.

Did not say a word. You were with the White lady who married Coach Van Damme."

"I hated that. I am so sorry Cashmere. I was not sure how you were going to react. It was a set-up date. I panicked when I saw you."

"You know I cried all the way home. I had to explain to the kids what had happened. They worked so hard to make me feel good about myself."

"Remember Cashmere, a couple of days later you snubbed me."

"Yes, I did. I felt you had moved on. Even when I saw you for the first time in a while, I had kept hoping you would come back to me. I thought you had moved on Geronimo."

"Remember when I told you how I felt when I saw Coach Van Damme touch your hand? I felt hurt, humiliated. I wanted to hurt him. I am so happy that time has helped with the pain that we both experienced. We should really thank Skyler for wanting to talk with us. That presented another opportunity to show that we could work it out. Thank you for accepting my invitation."

"Certainly, I feel we both have grown. Hopefully, I do not have to cry again, like when I cried all the way home that day. I hope I will not have to hear that song again."

"Cashmere, what was it? What was the name of the song?"

"Where Do Broken Hearts Go? by Whitney Houston. I could not stop crying so I changed the radio station. Another song came on that made me cry even more."

"What was that?"

"Let's Stay Together by Al Green. I was crying so hard. It was like a waterfall of tears rushed from my eyes until I could hardly see to drive home. I did not think to use a tissue or my shirt to dry my eyes. So, I wiped my tears with the back of my left hand. In doing that, I scratched my eye really bad because I had my wedding ring on. I had not taken my ring off, not even one day, because I was embarrassed that someone would ask me why I was not wearing my ring. Besides that, I was still hopeful that you would come back to me."

"Cashmere, I'm so sorry that I hurt you like that. I felt hurt too. Of course, I thought you were my soul mate; but after the children came, I felt like we were jail mates. I cried many times myself."

"Geronimo, it didn't occur to me that you were unhappy. Believe it or not, after I scratched my eye, I thought to myself and followed up with saying out loud, why do I still have this ring on? Why? Why? Why? You know. It did not help my marriage at all. He has someone else. Then I removed the ring from my finger. I took the tissue box that was in the glove compartment, removed a lot of the tissue, wrapped the ring up in the wad of tissue and placed it in the change compartment of my wallet. It was like reality had finally sunk in. And I was broken."

"What did you do with the ring?"

"I took it to a pawn shop in Mobile and sold it."

"I'm sorry that happened. I wish you had given it to one of our children."

"Why would you wish that? It did not work out for us. I would never have given that to one of them."

"Because that really was an heirloom from my momma. I did not tell you that Cashmere."

"Oh, my goodness! I did not know. All I ever knew was that your mother picked it out. I would never want to be so insensitive about something so precious to your family. I could not keep it because it would remind me of my failure, not the success of your parents' marriage and I do not know, maybe your grandparents' marriage. I am sorry. It's that my pain was so great. I'm so sorry."

"It's okay. I understand. So did the shop give you a good price?"

"I sold it for two hundred dollars. The owner told me it was only worth that amount. Was it worth more?"

"I don't know how much it cost Cashmere. Maybe it's still there."

"I doubt it. It has been about three years. It was a little place called Percy's Pawn Shop."

"Honestly, someone got a nice heirloom."

"Geronimo, I guess this date has been a cleansing for both of us. Do you think we can forget about all of the hurt we have experienced, in addition to the newly discovered fact, that I sold your family's heirloom?"

"Cashmere, it was really your ring when I gave it to you. You did not know. I should have told you. My grandmomma gave it to my momma. It was a simple ring. Momma added a ruby stone to it. When my momma gave it to me for you, I added a few diamonds around the ruby. In a sense, because she helped me pick out the diamonds, I used that choice of words. But it was beautiful to me. I thought you would love it. Didn't you like it? If you did not like it, I would have gotten you another ring."

"Geronimo, I liked the ring. It was so pretty. It was very fancy for me. I hardly wore any jewelry. That's it."

"Going back to your question. We can forget the bad things that happened if we work hard to forgive. Think positive. We gotta do that if we are to have a fresh, clean start." Geronimo believed that with all of his heart.

Cashmere said, "I hope so."

"Here is our Pizza. Good company and good food. So, I hope this will ease our pain from long ago."

Cashmere smiled, "Oh yes. Of course, it will mend a broken heart. I cain't wait to take a bite."

The pizza was as delicious as Cashmere had last remembered it. Food does have a healing power. So, as they took the last bite, Cashmere's phone rang. She hesitated to answer, but she looked at the caller id. It was Jasmine. As they began to talk, Geronimo paid the tab.

"Momma, hey how are you doing? Was thinking

about you. Are you relaxing?"

"Yes, I am. How are you honey?"

"I'm doing ok. Just thought I would call to say hello. I really thank you for what you and daddy did this past weekend. I think I am going to call him right after I talk to you. I hear noise in the background. What is that?"

"Oh, I stopped to get a pizza after work. It is a treat for me after a long weekend. I was on my way out. It was pretty good. So, let me call you back when I get home."

"Oh, ok momma. Talk to you later."

"Geronimo that was our daughter. Of course, you heard what I told her, so I better get on in. She is going to call you later."

Geronimo joked, "You handled it perfectly Cashmere. I hope I don't let anything slip out."

Cashmere pleaded, "Please don't. Please be careful."

"Sooner or later, we will have to tell them."

"I would rather that it be later."

"Ok. Let's go."

Jasmine gave her momma enough time to get home. By the time Cashmere put her purse down, the phone rang.

"Hey momma. Glad you made it home so quickly. I called daddy first. He seemed very tired. He told me he would call me tomorrow because he had to rest. I hope we did not wear him out."

"He was happy to host you all, just like I was. So, any news? How is school?"

"Everything is fine. How is Sam?"

"Thanks for asking. Sam and Malinda have postponed their wedding."

"Really, what happened?"

"The company that they were going to work for went on a hiring freeze. With the freeze, the company froze the offer they had extended to them. I think Sam and Malinda made a good decision to postpone the wedding until they had jobs. You know that's not really a big deal to cancel because it's only the two of them in the wedding."

"Oh momma, are they bummed out about it?"

"No. Actually, they are really calm. That means Sam will be at home until they get married. So will Malinda."

"So, daddy knows right?"

"Truth be told, I'm not sure if Sam got around to telling him. That happened on Tuesday. Today is Wednesday. So, what did you really call about?"

"I don't know. Just miss being at home. I had asked Skyler's dad to come to Sam's wedding, but he is going to check on his ex-wife. She has been sick. I do not know. I was thinking that Skyler should go with him. Now that the wedding date has changed, I think I will suggest that. I know he would want me to go. If he decides to go, I think he should take that trip alone, without me. What do you think?"

"Do you know how long his dad was going to be visiting her?"

"He told Skyler it would be during the winter break. I would want to come home for those days. Is that selfish because he came with me?"

"No, I don't think that is selfish. Skyler should go home with his dad. That would be a great gesture. Tell him about your desire to come home. It will work out."

"Okay momma. That is funny. When I found out more details about his parents, I thought it would be good for him to go try to get clarity on what he has learned about her."

"My little girl is growing up. That is a wonderful idea. Skyler will appreciate your suggestion."

"Thanks momma. I got to get up early in the morning, so I will say goodnight. I will let you know how it turns out. Please tell Sam that I'm sorry that happened; but I'm proud that they are being so practical about it."

Although Cashmere was deeply sorry for selling the Summers' family heirloom ring, that she clearly saw was the cause of her injured eye and her injured heart, she knew it was right for her to get rid of the painful memory. In fact, she could not dismiss her feeling guilty for her action because of her love for Geronimo.

Chapter 26

Geronimo woke up early with one thing on his mind, the ring that Cashmere had sold. He was able to find the telephone number and address to Percy's Pawn Shop. He almost called the shop when he thought to himself that it might be better to go to the shop and browse. If he called the shop, asked specific questions while giving the specific description of the ring, he might alert the owner that it was something very important to him, very valuable. If he left for Mobile, he could arrive by nine o'clock in the morning and be back at least by noon because it was only about a ninety-minute drive.

That is precisely what he did. He went to Mobile

and hoped for a miracle. He really did not turn the radio on because he wanted to meditate on potentially starting over with the love of his life. He reflected on their conversation at dinner, reasoning that the things both of them had learned and the heartache they experienced would make them better people, hence a better marriage partner. The drive seemed like it was only fifteen minutes when he pulled up into the parking lot of the modest shop in the little strip mall.

He analyzed the area and went into the shop. An older White gentleman greeted him and asked what he could help him with. Geronimo said that he was looking for something sweet to give to his daughter. He browsed through the earrings. Then the man asked him, "How old is your daughter?"

Geronimo answered, "She is eighteen years old, and she is playing basketball at the University of Alabama." The man seemed impressed and asked another question.

"Does she like watches or rings?"

"Seriously, she might like a ring. Don't want to pay a lot for it because she might lose it."

"Come over here and take a look at these rings I have in this area." As Geronimo browsed through the rings, he did not see the one that Cashmere had sold.

He asked, "Do you have any more rings? Something really simple. She's not a flashy girl."

"Oh yes, gotta few that I don't have out because I have had em so long until I put em away, so I could set out my newer inventory. Hold on a second. Let me get the other tray here." When he bent over to pull out the tray in the bottom drawer, Geronimo bent over to look at it. The man put the tray on the table and Geronimo began to look for his family's heirloom. He picked up several rings to examine them, only to discover that the ring no longer existed.

He said to the owner, "Well I don't see anything that she would like. Gotta keep on looking." About the time Geronimo said that his eyes went to a little antique pink baby doll with a large head. On the baby doll's neck was a long handkerchief with something holding the handkerchief in place. He slowly walked toward the baby doll.

The owner asked, "Do you think she would like the baby doll?"

"Possibly. She might. Let me look at it a little closer."

When he got closer, it was his family's heirloom, holding the large handkerchief in place on the baby doll's shoulder.

"This is something I think she might like. She could put it on her bed. How much is it?"

"You know, I have had that doll for a long time. Why don't you give me thirty dollars for it? It's a little beat up, but I kept it in case someone wanted it for a little girl."

"Can I examine it a little closer. It's hard to see on that shelf."

When the owner took it down from the shelf,

handed it to Geronimo, it was his momma's ring holding that thick handkerchief in place on the baby doll's neck and shoulder.

"So, sir, are you selling the clothes in addition to everything on the doll for thirty dollars?"

"Yeah. You know, come to think of it, since your daughter is at Alabama and I'm a fan of Alabama, you can have it for fifteen dollars."

"Thank you, sir. I'll take it."

The owner said, "You know what's so funny about that doll with all those clothes on?"

"No. What?"

"I remember the lady that came in here. She was a pretty Black lady. She was taller than me. Pretty hair. She had a pair of sunglasses on that covered her eyes and her eyebrows when she came in. You know, she eventually took them off. Her eyes looked tired. She talked in a very slow tone and her voice was shaking a little bit. She looked like her whole world had collapsed and that she did not have a friend in the world.

"She looked so pitiful. She told me she wanted to sell her ring because it made her so sad. So, I offered her two hundred dollars. Told her that was what it was worth. I thought it was worth a little more than what I told her; but I figured she did not want it anyway and if I did not get it, let's say buy it from her, she would just throw it away. I sort of hated to do that. You can understand my position. It was just business. She sold that ring to me for two hundred dollars. Nobody could tell me that I would not make a profit.

"What really got me was that no one even looked at it ever. So, I decided to dress up the baby doll, knowing that it could be a special gift for a young girl. I took a loss on that, but I'm happy you will have it for your daughter."

"Me too! I'm not sure when I am going to give it to her. I will keep it at the house. Maybe I can surprise her one day soon."

"Good. You do that sir. It was nice talking to you. It was nice doing business with you. Please come back again. Please tell your daughter I hope she has a good season. Go Alabama!"

Geronimo got in his car and drove back to Monroeville with Cashmere's ring. On the ninety-minute ride back, he now had more to walk down memory lane concerning his life. This was the first time he took note of his life in detail. That was because so many things were happening one thing right after the other. He started by wondering why his eye noticed the baby doll among so many other things that were in the shop. Puzzled by that fact, he soon remembered that his grandmomma had a guest room that no one had ever slept in but the mountain of different styles and sizes of baby dolls beautifully dressed. He thought to himself, how long ago that had been since he saw his grandmomma's doll collection?

He remembered when his grandparents' house

burned down because of an electrical problem. She was not able to save the collection of dolls. He recalled her crying, "my house, my dolls, oh my house, my house." When his grandparents rebuilt the house, she never collected dolls again. Geronimo did not remember those dolls until he saw the one in Percy's Pawn Shop. It was so peculiar to him how the subconscious mind could reveal or hide things from you. In the case concerning the dolls, he was quite happy that the dolls came back to his mind. Otherwise, he would not have gotten the ring back.

He also thought about the Clausell Community Center and how it was named after their family, and how taking the tour of Monroeville, especially the Clausell Community Center with the four kids from college reminded him of his heritage, as well as the many visits to the park with his Cashmere. He was thinking about how his great granddaddy was born a Clausell, and that he had a lot of land that he had inherited, two hundred acres. He gave Geronimo's granddaddy one hundred acres. Geronimo's granddaddy gave thirty acres of his land to his only child, Geronimo's momma. And out of the kindness of his granddaddy's heart, he gave Geronimo, his only grandchild, ten acres when he turned eighteen years old. His granddaddy told him not to sell it. And he laughed, "You never know what will happen. This town may change, and the value of the land may go up. You could sell the land, or you may need to build a house on it for your family. Then you could have room for a garden for food. Just do not do anything with it for a while. This could be your emergency go to fund for help."

He listened to his granddaddy's advice. Geronimo never did anything with it. He put it in a safe deposit box at the bank. He was able to do what his granddaddy wanted because he really wanted to play professional basketball. Geronimo loved the game of basketball. He ruptured his Achilles tendon when he was a senior in high school. Not one college team picked him up. His injury did not appear to be serious. But it was serious. He crashed.

His granddaddy had a small construction company. On top of that, he worked with his granddaddy on a few of the renovation projects during the summer. No matter what job his granddaddy had him to do, someone always asked him did he play basketball. The muscular six feet four inches tall eighteen-year-old got a lot of attention. His hair was wavy, with a little bit of fuzz to it. Still, few people ever noticed it because he always wore baseball caps over his short-cropped hair. His skin color was like the color of a dark chocolate bar. He was a very dynamic person with lots of energy. He attended the junior college in Monroeville where he studied Business Administration, while he was working with his granddaddy. However, before he graduated and started working as a free-lance bookkeeper, he met Cashmere on one of his granddaddy's renovation projects. He had never seen a girl that tall. She was five feet ten inches tall. Other than that, he only saw girls five feet two inches to five feet four inches. He felt she was the one for him. And they fell in love.

Then he started thinking about how everything was good at first. How he hated that their life got out of control after the children were born. He regretted how he walked away from the only girl he had ever loved. The truth is that because of his frustration of not reaching his goal, two dreams shattered, playing professional basketball, and being married till death. He contrasted how he looked almost twenty-two or twenty-three years later. He had some muscles, but not very defined. He had lost some of his hair. He was not as passionate as he was about life then. But above everything he contrasted, now how he had the opportunity to reconcile with Cashmere after being divorced five years. That made up for everything he felt sad about. Suddenly he recalled something that he had totally forgotten.

He was so busy trying to accommodate Jasmine's

friend Skyler, that he had forgotten about what had happened four days before they asked to come down for the weekend. Surprisingly, Geronimo's granddaddy called to tell him that they had found oil on their property, which would include Geronimo's property. How had he forgotten that? Simply put, Cashmere and his children had taken priority. He could see how he had changed, as well as, how he was still changing every single day.

When he said he wanted to take care of Cashmere, that she could do what she wanted with her money, the news about the oil had not even entered his mind. He was thinking of taking care of her on the money he made from his bookkeeping clients. Now he had to decide what he was going to do. Should he tell Cashmere about the ring or wait? Should he tell her about the potential to have found oil on the property or wait? He concluded that he should wait to find out more details. The ride home from Percy's Pawn Shop was a little more taxing than the ride down to Percy's

Pawn Shop. He had pretty much covered his entire life on the way back.

He made it back to Monroeville about a half hour later than he had expected. It did not matter because he needed the time to mull over his life. He went straight to the bank, putting the ring in his safe deposit box with the deed for the land his granddaddy had given him when he turned eighteen years old.

Geronimo had to pick up the receipts from one of his bookkeeping clients around four o' clock; therefore, he had some time to go to his grandparent's house for a brief visit. This was the first time he had visited them after they found oil on their land and by extension his land. His grandparents told him that they were driving through their land when they noticed that oil was on the surface of the ground. They suspected that there was something to this because they had a friend who had found oil on his land in one of the neighboring counties. They hired a geologist to come down from Birmingham,

Alabama to inspect the land. They found that oil was on the property. So, his grandparents were trying to figure out their next step.

His grandmomma said, "Honey, you know that means we are going to have to drill for oil. We do not know how much is there, but according to that team, we can start drilling because it is there. We wanted you to help us with the details."

"Grandmomma, I would be happy to help. But I don't know anything about digging for oil."

His granddaddy handed him the report. "Here is the report. You study it and if it turns out to be a lot of oil on the property, you might make a good penny."

"What about the thirty acres that you gave to momma? Is that included or is it only the ten acres you gave to me along with the remaining acres that you kept?"

"That's a good question. To tell you the truth, I don't know."

"It seems like it might be all of them acres; but my understanding is that it might vary depending on where they're drilling. That is why I want you to find out all of the basics. You can understand all that kind of stuff more than me. Put that young mind to work."

"I'll do my best granddaddy. Am I the only one that knows about this?"

"No, I told your momma that I was going to ask you to look into it. And for her not to say anything else about it yet."

"Okay granddaddy. I will read the report. Probably, will call the geologist to find out more. Then I will see if there is a book at the library or I might order one online to become more knowledgeable. Not sure how to approach this until I read all of this.

Thank you for the opportunity. I have some bookkeeping work to pick up this afternoon, so I will start on it tomorrow."

"That's fine by me Geronimo. Your grandmomma

and I realize that you have a lot to do. We really appreciate you taking on this task. Please keep us up to date. If we find out anything else, we will let you know. Talk to you later."

Geronimo left his grandparents' house. He went to his client's office to pick up the receipts so he could finish the bookkeeping. After he got home, Geronimo remembered to call Jasmine. She picked up the phone and shouted, "Hey daddy! I am glad you did not forget about me. How was your day?"

"Honey it was super busy. You know I would not forget about you. But I really wanted to find out why you called last night. Is everything ok?"

"Sure. Daddy everything is ok. Totally feeling like I needed to call home. Visiting with you and momma this past weekend just made me think about you two and I wanted to be home. So, we start basketball practice next week. Getting ready for the season, I know I need to stay focused. I talked to momma last night. She sounded happy although tired. Have you talked to her since we left?"

"Yes, I have. We talked about the visit we enjoyed with your friends. So, we are happy for all of you. Look forward to getting to know Skyler better. He is a nice young man. So, honey I wanted to touch base with you as I promised. I have some bookkeeping to do and some other things I need to take care of. I am sorry. I need to do it now. So call me anytime you need to talk. The fall season used to make you a little sad. This is your first year away from home. We know that starting to train for the season is going to release those good endorphins. Am I right?"

"Yes, you are right daddy. Thanks again for everything. You can call me whenever you want to. I will do the same. Talk to you later. Bye now."

Well Geronimo handled that call pretty good with Jasmine. He knew that he had to be on his toes when he was talking with her. Just asking a subtle question like 'Have you talked to momma since we left?' could have easily made him divulge sensitive information that he and Cashmere were not ready to release to anyone yet. Geronimo knew that he would need to limit the amount of time he talked to Jasmine because of her analytical mind. She could pick up something quickly. She could ask another question and another question until she had built a story. He was hoping that basketball would keep her busy.

Chapter 27

Geronimo finished the bookkeeping. His next task was to review the report that his granddaddy gave him. As he went through the report, everything looked good. However, reading it and understanding it were two different things. He read it; but could not understand it. He called the group that compiled the report. After speaking with them, Geronimo asked if the geologist could visit Monroeville and walk the land with them as he explained the report. The man agreed to do it. He set an appointment to come down on Friday afternoon at three o'clock.

Instead of calling his grandparents to tell them, he decided to go by and talk with them. His grandparents were surprised to see him along with this big box he brought with him. His granddaddy asked, "What do you have in the box?"

"Here. It's for grandmomma."

She said, "Well that is a surprise. What is it?"

Geronimo responded, "Grandmomma, it's something you used to do when I was a little boy."

She opened it. "Would you looka here. It is a baby doll. Where did you get this?"

"In Mobile. I saw it then thought about you. It is old but it still looks good. Why did you stop collecting baby dolls after the house burned down?"

"It's like this Geronimo. I did not think I could replace any of my children. Those baby dolls were like my children. How would I ever replace them."

"I know what you mean. I hope this gift does not make you sad."

"No, on the contrary, it's a pleasant surprise. I could dress her up plus put her on the shelf. Thank you, Geronimo. You gave me a nice surprise. I might start collecting dolls again. That's been about thirty years ago since I stopped collecting dolls."

"Yes. It has been. Also, the guy who drafted the report is coming down on Friday. It was hard to understand the report, although it was easy to read. We will go through it together. Then if you want to, you can come hear what he has to say. It might make a little more sense this time around."

"That's not a bad idea. Ok. We can do that. It's better to get as much information as possible."

"Ok. It will be at three o'clock on Friday. That will be good."

He gave his grandmomma a hug, his granddaddy a hug and left. After that, his grandmomma hugged the doll and said, "We got to get you cleaned up. Someone has neglected you. I'm going to show you how to dress."

Her husband was so happy to see her excitement. Geronimo didn't get the sense of his grandmomma's words when she said, 'I didn't think I could replace any of my children. Those baby dolls were like my children. How would I ever replace them.' His grandmomma had another baby five years after Geronimo's momma was born. The child lived for seven days then died. She was never able to conceive another child. In her sorrow, she started collecting dolls, becoming really involved with taking care of her baby dolls. Not that she had lost her mind. It was that she loved so hard. How could she replace her daughter?

Each time she collected a doll, it allowed her to keep her baby's memory alive, something she never wanted to forget. Of course, the death never made her bitter, being thankful that she had at least one child of her own. She kept that secret from Geronimo's momma, and of course, his momma could not tell him something that she did not know.

Since the gift was purely out of what he remembered about his grandmomma's collection of dolls, she could not bring herself to reject the gift.

Literally, she was more excited about the doll than knowing that oil was on their land.

The geologist came Friday for the three o'clock appointment. Geronimo and his grandparents got a chance to really understand what was involved. The meeting was successful. Without a doubt, there was oil on their land. The next step was to arrange for the drilling. Being simple minded people, they wanted to have one drill for starters. They would talk about more drills later, if necessary.

From entertaining college kids to partially reconciling with Cashmere to speaking with a geologist about oil on the Clausell property was a heavy week for Geronimo. The next thing he had to do was check-in with Sam to see how he was doing. Sam answered, "Hey daddy. What's up?"

"Checking in on you son. How are things for you?"

"Going ok daddy. Gotta find another job. I have been busy with that on my mind. Since Malinda and

I have postponed the wedding until we get jobs, I'm going to stay put at momma's house."

"When did that happen?"

"On Tuesday. I thought momma might have told you."

"No. Are you and Malinda ok with that?"

"Gotta be. Daddy I am in the middle of something now. Let me catch you later."

"Sure son."

Geronimo had one final call to make. He called Cashmere. She answered the telephone. Cashmere's Spa.

"Hey Cashmere, this is Geronimo. Your professional voice sounds delightful. I talked with Sam. He gave me the news about his job and the wedding."

"Yes, it's good he told you. I could have. Did you call him, or he called you?"

"I called him."

"That's even better. It's hard to read Sam right

now. But he seems ok. I will be able to tell more as this goes on. They probably will not get married before the summer. He wants to save some money. He also said Malinda was ok too. I told them that was the right thing to do. He could stay as long as he wanted. How was the rest of your week?"

"It was really busy. And yours?"

"Busy. I am totally thinking about adding another section to my business. A lot of my customers like the essential oils that we have in the massage area. So, I will start formulating different fragrances from the essential oils for deodorants, soaps, and lotions. I could make them as gift packages or sell them individually. What do you think?"

"You can do both. I think that is a great idea! Who do you have in mind to help you with that? I thought about Malinda and Sam. You know they mixed the shades of paint for my Spa, and they have a real artistic flair. And they can design the labels for each of the items. So, if they are interested, they could run that part of the business for me. It could possibly grow into a mail order business."

"I think that would be great for them. Would you be able to finance that additional part of your business?"

"I think so. Right now, it is a thought. I have not worked out the details. There is a room in the Spa that I have not used. It is a room that I throw everything in there that I am not using. I can start from there building my inventory."

"Sounds like I see a strong entrepreneur talking."

"Well, I'm trying. Are you looking forward to a busy weekend?"

"Sure Thing! It depends on a couple of things though. Whether you are available and what you would like to do."

"Cute Geronimo. When was the last time you worked out? Let's meet at the gym?"

"The gym? It has been a while. Is that what you want to do? Not eat Pizza?"

"That's fine. I can compromise. We can go to work out for an hour. Then stop in for a slice of pizza after the workout."

"Ok Cashmere. That sounds good to me. First comes the pain, then the glory."

"I like that. When do you want to go?"

"Sunday around three o'clock Cashmere because the gym closes at five p.m."

"That's perfect. Thanks for calling. I'll see you then Geronimo."

That call really encouraged Cashmere. She started reminiscing about their first date. How she dressed up. And it was so different to how life had been for her. She dressed up for work. Her spiritual service. But not much else. On her date with Geronimo, she wore a nice short sleeved yellowish green dress with bamboo accessories. Now on her second date, she would be going to the gym to sweat. Then after that Pizza. The gym did not have a shower. How would she dress?

She had been working out in unattractive clothing because she did not want to draw any attention to herself. She knew she had to go shopping at the Walmart. She had enough time to get a nice workout outfit that showed she was a lady. She headed to Walmart right after she got off from work.

She found a cute outfit that was not too flashy, nor to drab. It was perfect. Then she realized that she might need to pick up a few more outfits in case she bumped into Geronimo at the gym or in the event she saw him at the Community Center. Cashmere felt renewed.

On her way out of Walmart, she ran into Missy, Marylou's momma, coming into Walmart. While they were neighbors besides friends, both of their schedules had changed so much that they hardly saw each other. They talked briefly. Each kept on walking. Missy doubled back to tell Cashmere that they were thinking about moving to North Carolina and did not want her to be surprised. They needed a change. Cashmere noticed that Missy did not seem happy about it. She said, "We can talk later about that Missy."

Relieved by her response, Missy said, "Thanks Cashmere. It's too much to go into now."

"I understand Missy. We'll talk later."

They did not talk about it later.

Chapter 28

Cashmere and Geronimo met for their second date at the gym. Both were extremely excited to see each other. They could focus on themselves. Geronimo was waiting when Cashmere drove up. After the first date, he said to himself, "I would rather wait on her, than she having to wait on me." So, he arrived about twenty minutes before they were supposed to meet. When Cashmere drove up, she did not recognize that he was there. He had parked a distance away in a corner on the side of the building, where he could see everyone that drove up.

He watched her put something into the trunk. He saw her pick up her water bottle and her towel out of the trunk. When she got back into the car, she looked at her face in the rear-view mirror. He saw her tap her lips with a hint of lipstick. She flipped her hair and pulled it to the top of her head. She loved hoop earrings. He remembered that. She never went anywhere without two things on. She had to have her lipstick on and her earrings on. Nothing else mattered. About ten minutes more it would be three o'clock. He thought that she may have been checking the time when he saw her look at her phone.

She got out of the car, stood for a second, looked around and decided to get back into the car. So, when it was exactly three o'clock, she started walking to the front door of the gym. As she was walking and looking behind to see if Geronimo was driving up, he had gotten out of his car, unobserved by her, and sprinted to the door to open it. She fell out laughing.

"Where did you come from?"

"From the front side of the building. I have been here waiting on you. I wanted to watch you as you drove up. I wanted to see you get out of the car. When I saw you put some lipstick on, I remembered how you would always put your lipstick on and your hoop earrings on before you left the house. You would not leave home without those two things."

"Ahhh. I'm happy that you remembered that. I remember how you always tried to surprise me, even though I did not like surprises."

"Maybe that wasn't a good surprise then. But then again, there were some surprises that you did like."

"That's true. You are right. Like when you surprised me with a beautiful pair of hoops with a couple of dangly things at the bottom of the hoops."

"I remember that Cashmere. I wanted to do something unique for you; however, it was always difficult. But whenever I got you a pair of hoops, you would have thought I gave you a diamond watch."

"That's right Geronimo. Are you ready to go through your workout Geronimo?"

"My work out? I have not been to the gym in a

while Cashmere."

"You look like a buff forty-one-year-old to me."

He grinned. "Thank you. I am going to hold on to that compliment. What is your workout routine like Cashmere?"

"Routinely, I warm up for about five to ten minutes on the treadmill. Then I stretch a little bit. Maybe ten minutes. Then I head to the weights. Usually, I run laps on the track in between sets."

"All in one day?" Geronimo teased.

"Come on Geronimo. I know that you are kidding me. What do you want to do? My routine or your routine?"

"Let's do your routine Cashmere. Next time we can do my workout if I survive this." After they finished the warmup, Cashmere asked, "Geronimo, how did you feel when we got a divorce?"

"Cashmere, this may slow down our workout. Do you really want to talk about this now?"

"Sure, I do Geronimo. We have a lot to catch up

on. These are the type of things we never talked about after the breakup. So, I would like to know if that is all right with you?"

"Ok. I understand your question. But I would like to give you a little background that will help answer the question. My association was not the best while we were married. Even though the children sent me over the deep end, I was talking with my buddies, who told me this, 'if you are not happy and the marriage is too stressful, simply walk away. You should not have to be unhappy like this.' That was wrong advice they gave me and furthermore, I should not have told them that I was unhappy. They caught me at a very weak time. The kids were sick. We did not have money and I did not want any of my relatives to know about my struggles.

"As the children grew older, it was one thing or another. It never stopped. And I wanted them to have things that I could not afford. Every time I lost my job, I felt demoralized because there you were working, taking care of the kids, and trying to do your best to take care of yourself and me. I would say that I am not taking care of my family. What kind of man am I? Demoralized again and again, I always felt like I was a failure. And I kept comparing myself to others. Not good. Since then, I have learned that was a formula for misery.

"I knew I was wrong to leave my family like I did. Of course, I was selfish. The pressure was too great to stay. And it was even greater when I left. I could not catch a break anyway, shape, form, or fashion. I felt like you spent so much time with the children and there was no time for me. I was torn between feeling neglected and feeling trapped. And what is so funny about that is those feelings rotated. Trapped one day and neglected the next day. I could not break the cycle. The trapped part came from my friends, who were womanizers. They were not family men.

"By the way, my so-called friends left me when I left you. It was almost like I had been set up. When

I look back, they were not friends. They were haters. What friend would not help a friend to do the right thing?

"More specifically, here is how I felt after the divorce, I was too embarrassed to say I made a mistake. I hated who I was. I felt like a loser. I felt that others called me a loser. And I tried my best to avoid you. Several times I saw you before you saw me, and I hid. Yeah, I hid. Can you believe that? Looking at you made me see myself as I was, not as I wanted to be. Earlier, my so-called friends had pushed me to move on with my life. But my life was with my family. I did not know how to get back to my family. That is how I felt."

"Why didn't you call me, even if you feared my response, then it would have been on me if I had rejected you?"

"Cashmere, please listen closely. Any man who leaves his family is not mentally stable. I was not thinking logically. If I had been, I would have never left. How could I feel jealous about my own children? That is what it boiled down to. In fact, this is the most honest I have been with myself when you asked me that question. I like that you helped me to see that we could start off fresh. We could have dating rules that would help us know each other how we are now, not how we were, because clearly, we are two different people now. Does that make sense?"

"Yes, it does Geronimo. I really understand your feelings. I did not feel that I had your undivided attention. I had given birth to two children in two years. My body had changed. My looks had changed, and I felt unattractive. I dressed how I felt. No more red lipstick. No more hoop earrings because the babies would yank them. No more fitted clothes because I could not fit what I had, so I bought clothes that gave me a range of twenty pounds higher or lower.

"I was only twenty-one years old when we started having problems. I was barely a grown woman when

I began to act and dress like a grandmomma. I felt no one would understand because I didn't. I was not able to communicate my feelings. I did not feel that I was worthy of a night out without my children because now I was a mom and that was new for me.

"I wish I had thought about putting the children to bed and have a date in the house. Just like we danced with the children a couple of weeks ago, we could have had dates with the babies. What would have prevented us from laying the babies in their cribs right in the living room with us as we just talked or had a glass of wine? Nothing. Without a doubt, I let my insecurities about my appearance get in the way. We both felt horrible. I did not know how to handle it.

"This may blow your mind; but this is how far I had let myself down. I felt really bad when I would see you look at another woman, even if the woman who looked at you was old enough to be my grandmomma and a cashier at the Piggly Wiggly who gave you change back. I would feel sick to my stomach. If I told you that, I feared you would say I was being too sensitive. I yearned for sincere compliments. Yeah, your compliments were flattering, but not truthful to me because of how I felt. I could not deny how I felt when I looked at myself.

"You know, Geronimo when I think back to those days, I should have thought about you and your feelings. I kept putting my feelings first. Sometimes that does happen. I did it all the time because I was not happy with a lot of things, mainly me.

"One day, I was alone with the kids. You said you would be home early, and you did not come home until nine p.m. I had not showered. I had eaten only a handful of nuts. I was tired. I was sick. You were thoughtful because you called me several times that day. You asked me how my day was going; I told you that it was a very hard day. And you did not ask why or what happened. Obviously, you were not listening. I cried because I felt trapped. I could not leave with two children in my arms. I was too afraid to leave our bedroom. On top of that I had injured my foot and I could not walk.

"When you came in you heated up food, which I had cooked the night before. You told me you would call me on the phone when I could come take a shower because you needed to take one first. I was in the next room; yet you called me on the phone to tell me to do something else for you. How was I supposed to feel? I could not put the kids down and when I wondered what was taking you so long in the bathroom, you said that you had some things to take care of. What things? How was that possible? You had almost twelve hours alone I thought. I cried again and I went to sleep in the chair.

"I hurt so badly. And I tried to let the good you did for me be greater than the bad I felt about you. I kept telling myself that I chose you and you chose me, so this too shall pass. If you were afraid, how much more so do you think that I was afraid with two little kids, two little ones, depending on me. I prayed not to wallow in my sadness. I prayed not to wallow in my regrets, but to be thankful for what gifts I received. At one time, my husband seemed touched by my tears of joy; but later, he despised my tears of pain. I prayed not to wallow in what I would have done with my life, but to remember how much I had grown.

"Clearly, I was a different person. I was not the person I used to be. I knew deep down I would never be that person again. My emotional pain had almost rewritten what was originally my DNA, a happy, innocent Southern girl that loved life. I do not blame you now. Not at all. I did then. Now that is another example of how I felt once upon a time."

"Thank you so much Cashmere for the dignity that you have shown me, the forgiveness you have expressed to me. You have been what I have always wanted, more than that, you were what I needed. I hope that we never get to the point that we cannot talk about subjects like this. I do not ever again want to see you hurt because of me. I will do my best to protect you, love you and astonish you as much as I can."

"Thanks Geronimo. I'm a little wiser now Geronimo; yet, I have a lot more to learn. So, when I look at the facts, everyone has problems. I knew we loved each other, although I did not know how to love me, and you did not know how to love you when each of us was going through a trying time. I recognize that neither I nor you were competent to handle the problems we faced. The good thing is we now know that everyone needs good and helpful counsel. We should never ever try to be what we are not."

"Cashmere, I really agree with you. I told you that answering your question would slow our workout down and it did. You see our workout has been a good warmup. We did not have a drizzle of sweat Cashmere, not even a shine on our faces. By the way you look fabulous. I like your outfit. It is very modest, yet quite appealing. The color compliments your skin tone. Also, your hoop earrings, your pinkish red lipstick and your happy disposition is a nice flashback of the past. Your hips are still wonderful. I think you planned that soft workout so that we would not be drenched in sweat when we went to get a slice of pizza."

"I didn't plan it that way Geronimo, but I'm happy that it worked out that way. Well, I am hungry. Most of all, I feel a little more secure since talking to you about our past and our feelings. This conversation has proved to be excellent free therapy."

Cashmere got into her car. Geronimo got into his car. She followed him to the Pizza hut. This date would be a continuation of a soul-cleansing when they arrived at Pizza Hut. They went to the same table and ordered the same Pizza as last time.

"Geronimo, thank you for convincing me that you really wanted to be with your family. I really believe you with all of my heart. My experience with you on these two dates has helped me to understand what you were going through. A lot of times, women do not think of men as having feelings because we may believe what we have heard. 'All men are dogs.' I know that not all men are dogs. Men have feelings. Men do fall in love. A label that men put on women is all women have attitudes. That is not true. And now not only do we have the opportunity to apply what we have learned, but also to be a source of encouragement for our children. They will need us. Because of what we went through, we can help them if they come to us. You know it is a fine line in trying to help and being a busy body in our children's lives. They will have challenges. And I want to be available for them and inspire them to be thinkers. Do you agree with that?"

"Yes, I agree with that. Cashmere, I think that this is beautiful. I never thought I would have the opportunity to be a part of Sam and Jasmine's life to this extent when I left. And to think that Skyler started all of this in motion. It is starting to feel like I can put my regrets behind me and move forward with being a positive influence in my family's life. Thank you for giving me the chance to make it up."

"Geronimo, you know, the children have never thought of you in a negative way. Of course, they wanted to see more of you, like every day when they were tweenagers. They always hoped that we would get back together. So, I feel confident they can put their little regrets behind them because you are active in their lives as you have always been. Our timing is perfect. Both of our children are about to make some heavy decisions that will affect the rest of their lives. I'm happy we are available to help them."

They finished the Pizza and set up a date to have pizza every Sunday at five p.m. In that way, they could do their own workout. Moreover, Cashmere would not have to worry about going out to eat right after the workout with sweaty clothes.

Chapter 29

Basketball season started. The lineup was interesting. Both men and women's basketball teams were winning. Geronimo, Cashmere, Sam, and Malinda went to a few games that were off the chart. Jasmine was doing well. They could see the other side of her. She was not struggling at all. She was a natural athlete with honed skills. They also went to see a couple of Skyler's games. He was like Jasmine. Focused. Their coaches had good things to say about both of them. As the season was winding down, Skyler asked Jasmine to go with him and his dad to visit his mother for a few days. That was reasonable because earlier she thought it would be the entire break; however, she had not considered that they would still be playing basketball.

Jasmine called Cashmere to tell her that she had accepted the invitation to go with Coach Chadsworth and Skyler to Florida for a few days. Jasmine reminded her mom that she had never met the woman that gave her that beautiful hope chest. She also called her daddy to tell him of her decision. He was okay with it because he had talked with the coach several times and had spent time with Skyler. However, he did not know about the hope chest that Mrs. Chadsworth had given to Jasmine, who in turn, gave it to her momma.

Cashmere told Jasmine that she had a gift of oils to send to Mrs. Chadsworth. She also knew that she had been living in a mental institution. She researched various oils and found out what would be good for someone going through major depression. She got this beautiful gift set all ready for Jasmine and sent it to her to give to Mrs. Chadsworth. Then she prepared one for her daughter and sent it along with Mrs. Chadsworth's gift. The three of them flew down to Sarasota-Bradenton airport and rented a car.

Mrs. Chadsworth was about forty-five minutes away from the airport. She had gotten up early enough that day to receive her visitors. Since she had not met the girl that Skyler was crazy about, she wanted to be full of energy and not look depressed. She worked to put forth her best effort.

She took her hair down from the ponytail, shampooed it with her favorite shampoo, Awapuhi by Paul Mitchell, and The Conditioner by Paul Mitchell. She had used those products for years when she wanted to wear her hair down because she got consistent results for her fine textured hair. Then she lightly put on her lipstick, and mascara. She finished by putting on a string of pearls with a teal-colored dress. Afterwards, she sat in her wheelchair, waiting for her guests to arrive.

Mr. Chadsworth walked in first, greeted his ex-wife

and hugged her. Behind him was Skyler. Skyler's height hid Jasmine. So, Skyler walked into the small room, greeted his momma, and hugged her. While he was hugging his momma, Jasmine walked into the room, greeted her, and handed her the gift. Mrs. Chadsworth accepted the gift.

She said, "Thank you. Who is this from?"

Jasmine said, "It's from my momma. My momma likes essential oils and she thought you would really like the assortment she put together."

Looking surprised, she replied, "Your momma? How do I know your momma? Is she from here?"

"No, Mrs. Chadsworth you don't know my momma. She's from Alabama."

"My son told me about a girl he met from Alabama that he liked, but she was from a small town like Monrovia, I think.

"Yes mam. It is Monroeville. My momma is from Monroeville and so am I."

"So, are you a friend of Skyler's girlfriend?"

"Ms. Chadsworth, you gave me a beautiful hope chest three years ago. Don't you remember?"

"Yes. Three or four years ago, I remember giving a hope chest to a girl named Jasmine."

Jasmine smiled, "Yes. I'm Jasmine."

"I didn't know you were a Black girl. Skyler never told me I was sending my beautiful, precious, hope chest to a Black girl."

Obviously embarrassed, Skyler scolded his momma. "Momma why did you say that? You know it has never mattered to me about color and I know that it has never mattered to you about color. Why now has your view changed? You are embarrassing me and Jasmine. I told you she was a beautiful girl. I didn't see the need to tell you she was Black."

"Well son, there is a need now because I had a bad experience with a Black man. I committed adultery against your daddy with a Black man. I worked with him at the school. So, I never was able to forgive myself. I finally had a nervous breakdown. And now you tell me your girlfriend is Black? All this time, I did not know that. Luke, did you know?"

"Yes, I did Liz. She is a basketball star at Alabama. How can you hold her color against her? Did she make you do what you did, commit adultery? I never held what you did against you. I always knew I was at fault."

"Luke, if they got married, every time I looked at her, I would think about what I did. That's too much to bear."

Jasmine did not waver when she gave her compelling reply. "Ms. Chadsworth, out of all due respect. I do not hold it against you, Skyler, or Coach Chadsworth, that I do not know my Great Aunt because see she left town alone, after having a relationship with a White man, who was her boss, and gave birth to his baby.

"I learned from my parents that everybody makes mistakes. Now if you cain't forgive yourself, you will never be able to forgive anybody else. So, can you please stop the madness?

"Your husband and your son love you very much. I even love you for what you did for me. My momma even loves you for what you did for me. I hate this one-time affair with a Black man broke your heart. Seriously, I am so sad for you. Not because of that long time ago affair, but for robbing yourself of a good family and robbing yourself of happiness.

"My momma worked hard to put this gift together for you. She told me to tell you thank you. That was so kind of you to give her daughter something that she could not afford. Right now, I do not want to disturb you anymore. I hope you heal yourself from your mental illness and your prejudice illness. I would not say what you said to me, to my worst enemy. Please, have a good day and I am not looking forward to seeing you ever again."

Jasmine walked out. Skyler tried to stop her, but she pulled away and told him that she would wait for them in the lobby. When he came back to the room, he looked at his mother with disdain.

He said, "Momma, everything she said was right. How could an eighteen-year-old be so wise momma? Tell me. Do you know? Well, I will tell you. She is not a coward. You are a coward. I do not get along well with cowards. I have met her entire family. They took me in a few days when a group of us visited with Jasmine in her hometown. And you say that to her? Your pain is beyond repair. Daddy has always said he would marry you right away. Obviously, you must not be telling him the whole truth. Otherwise, you would not have just done this horrible thing to Jasmine. Daddy, I cannot look at momma any longer. I will wait in the lobby with Jasmine."

Skyler found Jasmine rocking in a rocking chair. He asked, "Are you okay?"

"Yes, I'm ok. I am so happy I came. There is something else behind her prejudice. She is acting like a little girl who may have had a crush on a little boy, and it turns out the boy is interested in another little girl, but he was pretending to like the first girl who has a crush on him, just to get a piece a candy in her lunch bucket. And once he gets the candy, he returns to the little girl who he really likes. Then, your momma might be angry with the world because she was not submissive to your daddy when she should have tried to keep her family together. When two people get married, they should stick together.

"Your daddy has admitted his mistake, but not her. I hate that you had to endure the conversation that I had with her. I am not a coward. I am a fighter, and I am happy she was not my age. I could not let her tell me what she wanted to, trying to make me feel worthless, or blame me for being Black. She disrespected me and everyone in that room. She needed to know what kind a person that I am. I speak the truth. I am not afraid like when I first met you. Seeing how my parents tried to keep their personal feelings aside, now makes me proud of them."

Then someone said, "You should be proud of your

parents." Jasmine looked around. It was Mrs. Chadsworth. She was not in that wheelchair. She had walked down to the lobby. Now she was standing in front of her son and Jasmine.

"Jasmine, you have been the first person not to baby me. Everything you said was true. I was holding the complete truth from Luke. It was not a mistake that I had this relationship with this Black man. He is not nameless. His name is Joe. Skyler, it was to teach your daddy a lesson; but it backfired. And yes, I used Joe, not knowing at the time he was using me. The Lord said vengeance is mine, I shall repay. I took matters into my own hands. It got out of control. Please forgive me.

"Minutes ago, Luke asked me to re-marry him and move to Alabama. I have accepted his proposal. Jasmine you showed me that I have a lot more to work on. Yes, I was angry with Luke and Joe and myself. I do not know anything more to say when I see an eighteen-year-old call a grown woman out. Seriously,

I am proud of you. You are right when you say, 'you have robbed your family of happiness.' Will you help me get a few things packed? I would like to talk with you some more.'"

Jasmine asked, "Are you sure? There is no turning back."

"No turning back." She reached over to hug Jasmine.

It was an unforgettable moment. Skyler was speechless. His mouth was wide open. He could not believe that his momma could really walk. She had used that wheelchair for a crutch for such a long time. Tears were running down his cheek. His nose turned red because of wiping his face. His heart was thumping so hard. He thought it would burst out of his chest. All of this happened because Jasmine was not a coward.

His momma said, "I'm not going to be a coward any longer. I am sorry for what I have done to you Skyler and you too Luke. I am ready to change. I see

I need help to do that. Thank you for your patience. Since I gave you my hope chest Jasmine, one day I hope you will be my daughter-in-law."

That day, Jasmine needed the type of recognition that goes to a doctor for healing a patient. She healed Ms. Chadsworth with words of truth. Having Mrs. Chadsworth do an about face, showed the power of helping a person to tell the truth, to reason, to forgive, and to love was extraordinarily powerful.

After they finished packing, Ms. Chadsworth checked herself out of the mental institution that she had checked herself into one year ago. They all went to her home and gathered a few more things. Instead of staying in Florida that night, they were able to switch their flights and they returned to Alabama. Skyler sat with Jasmine. Coach and Ms. Chadsworth sat together, holding hands the entire trip. Love produced a good outcome because Mrs. Chadsworth was able to forgive herself and accept her husband's forgiveness. He was so happy that he had never stopped loving her. Not only that, he was happy that Jasmine decided to make the trip with he and Skyler to Florida.

When they arrived in Alabama, Coach Chadsworth checked his ex-wife into a nice hotel. He told her to pamper herself and that they would complete the marriage certificate the next day, get it notarized and take it to the probate court for recording. Following that, he dropped Jasmine and Skyler to their dorms. His last stop was at his apartment. Never did he think that this trip would be the turning point for his wife. What a day.

Coach Chadsworth did not waste any time. The following day, he picked Liz up from the hotel. What had happened the previous day turned back the hands of time. She looked beautiful and well rested. The burden that she had been carrying for over ten years was lighter than a feather after Jasmine's heroic reply. She and Coach Chadsworth completed the online Marriage Certificate and took it to his bank to get it notarized. Then they went to the probate court to have it recorded. In one day, they were married.

After Coach and Mrs. Chadsworth dropped the document off for recording at the Probate Court, State Law in Alabama married them. No blood tests. No marriage license needed. It was a done deal. Coach kissed his bride, and they went back to the hotel he had put her in the night before. Following their stay at the hotel, he took his wife to his apartment the next day. No one guessed what the outcome would be for the three-day trip that Coach, Skyler, and Jasmine had planned. Mrs. Chadsworth called Skyler to let him know that she and his daddy remarried and were at his apartment. Skyler called Jasmine to let her know what happened and Jasmine called her mom to let her know what happened on the trip.

This is what Jasmine said, "Hey momma. How are you? We are back. It was an interesting trip. We came back the same day we left. In short, Mrs.

Chadsworth was surprised that I was Black."

Jasmine told her momma the entire story. Cashmere was amazed all of that happened in three days. She told her daughter how impressed she was that she spoke up. Cashmere asked Jasmine if she could tell her daddy that story.

Jasmine said, "By all means momma. Please tell him. Because the same thing can happen with you and daddy. I saw how you two danced together. How neither one of you had any animosity in your bones. So be open to the possibility that you two could get back together."

"I will Jasmine. Listen, I hope the rest of the season goes well. I am proud of you. Momma has got to go now."

Cashmere could not believe how Jasmine, although young, was able to reason with Mrs. Chadsworth like an experienced woman. She could not wait to call Geronimo. He picked up on the first ring.

"Hey Cashmere. How are you doing? Tell me

some good news."

"Hey Geronimo. I was on the phone with Jasmine a few seconds ago. Skyler's parents remarried. Our young lady showed courage by telling Mrs. Chadsworth that she was missing out on sharing a beautiful life with her husband and son because of one mistake.

"Jasmine told me that we should be open to getting back together. She went on to tell me how she watched us at the little dance off. We carried ourselves like we loved each other. She's watching us."

"What do you think Cashmere? Do you want to tell our children that we have started dating?

"Yes. Tell them Geronimo. It would be another example of being a good forgiver. Some people tend to hold grudges, especially older ones. Not saying young people do not hold grudges. It is that they see life a little different than older ones. Certainly, they have more to do than to rehash decades of injuries."

"You are so right Cashmere. Everyone makes mistakes. If we do not forgive each other, it will lead to bitterness. There is no room in a marriage for competition or bitterness. Marriage should function as cohesive teammates not bitter rivals."

"You spoke like a true athlete Geronimo."

"You know that you had a legitimate reason not to extend forgiveness to me Cashmere. We are sending a positive, yet silent message that although this is not a perfect world, no one should get a divorce for the smallest infraction. If possible, try to reconcile. Make your marriage work. I've wanted to tell my children along with the world that I'm getting my baby back!"

"Oh Geronimo. Geronimo. One day I will ask your momma why she named you Geronimo."

"She'll tell you, that I was ready to get out of her belly to see her. I wanted to tell the world that she was my momma. And that one day, I was going to marry a girl named Cashmere."

"I have to go Geronimo. Talk to you later."

That later turned into thirty minutes. Geronimo called back because he felt exhilarated that Skyler's parents had remarried after all of those years because an eighteen-year-old had the courage to speak the truth. And she was their daughter.

This is what he said to Cashmere. "I love you. You love me. We have forgiven each other, and we have grown. I want you to be my wife. Do you want to be my wife? If so, let's get married today."

Cashmere replied, "Why did you wait so long to ask me?"

Before taking her words to mean yes, he said, "That means you accept?"

"Yes, I accept. We can tell the children that we are dating. Is that all right with you that we let the husband and wife down the street from me help us with our spiritual counseling?"

"I think that would be wonderful. Let's make an appointment to go to their house. I can talk with the husband. I really would like that. Let's wait until after the basketball season ends because it is almost over. When we get married, we can include the kids. I love you so much Cashmere. I want to spend the rest of my life with you."

"I love you Geronimo. I have never stopped loving you. We have a lot to look forward to. I am so happy. I look forward to our weekly Sunday dates. I hope they will never end."

"We have learned that we must keep the fire burning. I will work hard to keep our dates going. A date can be right at home. We could dress up and have ultimate privacy."

Cashmere did not waste any time. She went to her neighbor's house and knocked on the door. The neighbor invited her in.

Cashmere said, "My ex-husband and I are getting married after being divorced five years. We were young and did not know how to solve problems, so we divorced. I told him that you answered a couple of spiritual questions that I had, and we agreed that we needed counseling. He wants to meet your husband. We hope that we can schedule time to start our spiritual counseling. How much would that cost?"

"It's free. We received freely. We give freely. Please print your name and your ex-husband's name here with each of your telephone numbers. My husband will give him a call to set it up. I am happy you stopped by. Would you like a cup of tea?"

"Yes, I would. Thank you."

"So, Cashmere, do you have children?"

"Yes, I have two. My daughter is eighteen years old. She plays basketball for the University of Alabama. My son's name is Sam. He is twenty years old. He is an artist. Do you have children?"

"Yes, we have two children also. Two boys. I have a forty-five-year-old son whose name is Wilson. He is married with one child. My youngest son is forty-one. He is not married. How is your tea Cashmere?"

"It's good. Thank you. Ms. Hattie how long have

you been married?"

"Well, let's see. He says we been married longer than I say because he said I was going to be his wife on our first date. He was so funny. To answer your question, we have been married forty-nine years. We have had some challenges. We have never argued and never went to bed angry."

"I wish I had come to talk to you a while ago Ms. Hattie."

"Oh, that's sweet Cashmere. I'm happy you came today."

Ms. Hattie looked down at the paper. "Please tell Geronimo that my husband's name is Daniel. He will be giving him a call. Let me write my number down for you and my husband's number down so you can call me whenever you want to or stop by if you want to chat."

"I appreciate that. I know I will have a lot more questions. Ms. Hattie, thank you for the tea. I better get up and let you enjoy your day. I will talk to you soon."

"You already made my day." Ms. Hattie smiled.

Cashmere called Geronimo to let him know that she had spoken with her neighbor and that her husband would be willing to introduce himself and set up a time to meet. Cashmere's initiative motivated Geronimo. He was amped up. He knew that Cashmere was as excited as he was to start all over again.

Chapter 30

Cashmere and Geronimo met for their third date at the Pizza Hut. Geronimo told Cashmere that he had some good news, but he was waiting for the right time to tell her.

He began with this explanation, "When I graduated from high school, my granddaddy gave me some land. He told me to keep it. Do not sell it. So, I put it in a safe deposit box. I never touched it. He told me the property value could go up. I could make some money, or I could build a house on it or have a farm. But he stressed that I should not touch it. So, I forgot about it, in a sense.

"When the kids wanted to come down, do you remember I told them that it had to be the week they called, because I had something planned?" Cashmere nodded.

"My granddaddy had called a meeting. But again, I forgot all about it because I was so happy to reunite with you and visit with the kids. After they left, I remembered to call my granddaddy to find out what was going on. You will never guess what happened?"

"What happened?"

"Please guess."

"Okay, someone wants to buy it."

"No, guess again."

"Someone stole it from you?"

"No. Come on Cashmere."

"How much land did he give you?"

"Ten acres."

"Ten acres? They wanted to build a plant."

"Close. Are you ready?"

"Yes, Geronimo. I'm ready."

"There is oil on the land."

"What? How is that possible?"

"I don't know. But I met with the geologist last week. He confirmed that oil was on the property. He does not know how much but my granddaddy wanted one rig to drill for oil. My granddaddy had about two hundred acres. He gave some to my momma and gave me some.

"Remember? I was working for my granddaddy in the summer when I met you. I did not think about that land then. I was sad because I was not going to be able to play college basketball. Something always kept me distracted, so that I would not remember it or touch it. Old saying 'out of sight, out of mind.' The company from Birmingham will start drilling in a few weeks or earlier. My granddaddy wants me to help him since I'm the only grandchild.'"

"That is great Geronimo!"

"It appears that the geologist thinks it might be oil in other places on the land. My granddaddy is taking it one step at a time."

"That is exciting for your grandparents."

"Contrary to what you think, they had not truly thought about it that much. In fact, I gave my grandmomma a doll because she used to collect them. She was more excited about the doll than the oil. Isn't that interesting?"

"Yes, it is. Why was she so excited about the doll?"

"When I was a little boy, she collected dolls. The house burned down. She never collected them again. So, I thought she would like it. It was an antique baby doll. I learned that after my momma was born, it was another five years before my grandparents had another baby. And that baby died at seven days old. So, my grandmomma started collecting dolls to always remember her baby, who had died. She never told my momma that and that's why I did not know it."

"Where did you get the doll?"

"I got it from Mobile."

"I didn't know you went to Mobile for business."

"Yes, and I found what I was looking for."

"I wanted to show you something that you

described to me. Geronimo pulled out five to ten tissues that were folded and handed it to Cashmere."

She looked at him before she unfolded it. "What is this?"

"Look at it please." She opened the tissue and there was the heirloom engagement ring that he had given her.

"What? Where did you buy this? Where did you find this? Is this the one that I sold, or did you have someone to duplicate it?"

"This is the one you sold. I looked up Percy's Pawn Shop and I went to Mobile. I told him I was looking for something for my daughter and he showed me a few items and then he pulled out a tray of rings. It was not there in the tray of rings. I told him that I did not think that he had what I was looking for and when I turned around, somehow, my eyes went up and there on a shelf was this doll staring at me. Around the dolls neck was a scarf. The ring was holding the scarf.

"The owner remembered everything about you. How you looked. I would remember you too if I saw you; but it was your solemn emotions that you displayed and what you said about how the ring made you feel. He painted a word picture that was distressing to me. To hear the owner state that you were so sad tore me up. He told me that he gave you two hundred dollars for the ring and that he knew it was worth more than that; yet no one ever looked at that ring. For that reason, he used the heirloom to dress up the doll and put it on a shelf for a little girl. I couldn't bring myself to say I was the one who made you sad, the one who vowed to love you."

"Are you serious? Did he really say those things?"

"Yes, he surely did say that. To repeat the rest would be more than I can handle right now. And with what we have talked about lately, I knew he was telling the truth. How could a stranger see, what I could not see?"

"Geronimo, please put that behind you. We are

moving forward. In a sense that is what the name Geronimo means. We are excited about our future."

"Thanks Cashmere. You are right. Well on my way home, I remembered why my eye went right to the doll, so I gave it to my grandmomma. This is the family ring that you can pass down to Jasmine. Here is the ring for you to wear. Will you marry me again?"

He showed her an opened box with a ring that was a simple solitaire diamond. She looked at it.

"It's larger than the other ring."

"If you don't like it, we can get another one."

"I love it. I love the simplicity."

Geronimo put it on her finger.

"Once more, will you marry me again and accept this ring as a token of my love for you?"

"Yes, I accept the ring as a token of your love. Yes, I will marry you again. And yes, I will give this heirloom to Jasmine. I think Jasmine would wear it."

"I have a surprise. It is something that Jasmine gave me. Skyler had suggested that his momma give

Jasmine her hope chest because she did not have any daughters. I had encouraged Jasmine to accept it, but she did not want to because I had made one for her that she liked. Finally, she accepted it with the intentions of giving a little party to surprise me because I never had a hope chest. The day you saw me all dressed up, you asked me what was going on. Did I have someone else in my life? I replied, Me. That evening Jasmine gave me a party. She put a few items in the chest, a journal, a set of handkerchiefs and an envelope that was labeled, **DO NOT OPEN UNTIL YOU HAVE SET A MARRIAGE DATE**. I peeked into the envelope last night. Sam had drawn some pictures around the writing of three important statements to say to your mate. Would you like to guess what they were?"

"Sure. I love you. I love you. I love you."

"Close. I love you. I am sorry. Please forgive me."

"Our kids are thinkers Cashmere."

"In other words, Geronimo, since we are planning

to get married, we will need to say these things more than anything else we will ever repeat. That has been in my chest for three years. It has so much meaning. And think, Jasmine was only fifteen years old when she wrote that. I'm so happy that I did not cheat and open the envelope."

"I cain't believe that she discerned those things would contribute to a happier marriage."

"Consider this Geronimo. It doesn't take long for a child to see what needs to be done when they see what went wrong. Think about it. If we had said those things so much more, it would have helped. I can imagine Jasmine thinking, momma say I'm sorry and be done with it, or daddy say I love you and watch momma calm down."

"Cashmere, I can add a few more things to her list, like thank you, you look nice, I'm happy that I married you, I have never met anyone like you. Well, the basketball season will be over soon. So, we have a lot to decide."

"Like what? What are you thinking about?"

"What type of wedding ceremony if any? Where will we live? What will we do with our homes? When will we tell the children?"

"For sure. I would not mind having a simple wedding with the children and a few close friends. Another house denoting a new start. It doesn't matter to me."

"We can start working it out. We only have a short period of time left."

Not long after that conversation, Cashmere and Geronimo called Jasmine and Sam to tell them they were getting married three weeks after the basketball season ended.

After that, they started the spiritual counseling with the couple down the street as they had agreed they would do before they got married. Those sessions proved to be better than what they thought. They could not believe what they were learning and not only that, it was so pleasant. It was what they needed over twenty years ago. After six weeks of going to counseling twice per week, for an hour, they decided to continue after the wedding was over.

Chapter 31

Things started moving rather quickly for Geronimo and Cashmere. They found a four-bedroom house that they bought. It was about three miles outside of Monroeville. The drill was pumping a lot of oil from Geronimo's land. Cashmere's Spa was doing quite well with the expansion of her new line of handmade soaps, deodorants, and lotions that Sam and Malinda were making. Jasmine's team had completed the season with only three losses. Skyler's team completed the season with five losses. And as soon as they finished the season, they moved on to the next big event, Jasmine's parents' wedding.

Everything was prepared for the wedding. The

new house was beautifully decorated. The backyard had been perfectly landscaped. Cashmere and Jasmine had an appointment at her Spa to get their hair done, a facial, and a massage.

On the drive home, after their three-hour pampering session, Jasmine asked, "Momma, what do you think brought you and daddy back together to the point of getting remarried?"

"Honey, it started with Ms. Hattie. I asked her a question about marriage. Something that I had heard at the spiritual service with your friends. She helped me to see from the Holy Book that Geronimo and I could get back together. Jasmine, I really did not know when I was younger that a ring does not make the marriage. Ms. Hattie helped me to see from the Holy Book where the first marriage was performed."

"Momma, does that have to do with what you put in my hope chest and what Marylou's momma put in her hope chest?"

"Yes, you are exactly right."

"My momma never taught me the role of a wife. So, I have not been able to teach you that until now. Your father said the same thing. He did not fully know what the role of the husband was. He guessed what it could be; but he was a long way off. Your daddy said that he really appreciated the spiritual counseling for the role of the husband. He was thrilled that he was getting a formula for success."

"That's so good to hear momma. I'm so happy I asked you that question."

"Yes, me too. You see Jasmine, doom was all around us from the beginning. Neither one of us knew how to prepare from a spiritual point of view to have children, nor the effect that it would have on our marriage. We did not understand how both of our values would change in a short period of time.

"Your father said that the challenges he had, and the anxieties of life robbed him of understanding the affection, the compassion, the time, and the patience that I needed as his wife. You see, the money, the house, the travel, the food, the oil and the ring, all of these material things and much more can enhance a marriage; however, it also can divide a marriage."

"Momma, I can see that. I have been thinking about how many celebrities who look like they have everything together, and they have these thorny problems. They have to a larger degree what some people have, which is money; and yet, money does not solve a lot of the problems. I can see that. It must be more than about the material things, even though, there are some rich people are able to experience a long happy marriage. I really don't want to get caught in that trap when Skyler and I make pros and we get married."

"Jasmine what we learned is that there is a third cord that holds a marriage together. That third cord comes from the Creator of marriage. This cord is like a vine that produces tasteful fruit. As long as that fruit stays attached to the vine, it receives nourishment and growth. A husband and wife are like the fruit that comes from the vine if they stay connected. Even if they make a mistake, the Creator could graft them back into the vine. Then they could produce life and bear seeds. If there is a disconnect like our flesh, we began to wither and fall. You see, your father and I did not know that before we started dating the first time.

"Honey I want you to understand the purpose of marriage before you say I do. Most of the people in the world get divorced because they are ill-prepared. And that is what happened to me and your daddy. Fortunately, he never fell in love with another woman, and I never fell in love with another man.

"That is what I want for my children, to be well prepared for marriage and for life. Now, your daddy and I have promised to keep external enhancements in their place, but to work at caring for one another in a way that shows genuine love."

"That's a hit. Momma can Ms. Hattie study with me too?"

"Jasmine, you have a car that you can drive while you are in college. Let me ask you a question. If there is a problem with one of the major parts of the car, who would be the best source to get exact information about the car?"

"The person who made the car. The manufacturer."

"Correct. So, you want to go and talk to Ms. Hattie because she gets her insight from the Creator of Marriage. It is only one source. I think you will benefit, if you take the time to ask all of your questions that you could think of. One of the reasons that is so important is in the world today, there are so many schools of thought. For instance, there are millions of people who love to sample the fruitage of marriage which should be a sacred privilege; but they choose not to invest into the legal responsibilities of marriage privileges. And it will be proper for you to find out why. The fruitage of marriage should be a delicacy.

"Jasmine that is one of the most important investments that you could make towards marriage. Unexpected issues that you would never imagine could continue to challenge your marriage and every marriage union. If you keep up with current events, you will notice that more than sixty percent of marriages fail. I am sure we, your daddy and I, are in that number.

"Many people do not get married because they fear the unknown. To become one with your marriage mate is one of the most beautiful and respectful choices that you could make. You would potentially keep a clean conscience. And that would lead to a happy family life.

"I really feel Sam and Malinda will receive help from a study session too. But that is their choice. We all have free will. Your daddy and I have surely received help from this counseling, and although it was late, it was not too late. That is why there is going to be a wedding tomorrow with my children present.

Jasmine and her momma stayed in one part of the house and Geronimo and Sam stayed in another part of the house as they prepared for the next day. They all went to bed early and got up early.

Their wedding was different this time because their guests would arrive within two hours to a computer screen. It would be a zoom wedding. When Jasmine expressed to her parents that some of the students from her college had gotten sick from the Covid-19 virus, she then suggested that her parents not put her great grandparents at risk; thus, they scheduled a zoom wedding.

Among the guests invited were the Chadsworth Family, Geronimo's grandparents, Geronimo's momma, Malinda Fox and her parents, The Marshall Family, the Parish Family, Lillie Gray, Tommy Van Damme, co-workers from the flower shop that Cashmere worked with, staff from Cashmere's spa and Geronimo's client. It was a total of thirty-four guests that would be attending the wedding by zoom.

The wedding would last twenty minutes, including the vows. Cashmere was so excited about one gift they received before the wedding ceremony. Geronimo's grandparents gave them a one-month honeymoon vacation to Maui at Kapalua resort so they would be free of all distractions. They would have a true chance to get to know each other in another way. They had never been to Hawaii before. Now Cashmere realized they would get a chance to hear their heartbeat.

Everything about that day would take your breath away. It was a simple, but elegant country wedding. Cashmere and Geronimo said their wedding vows. Geronimo started off first.

He said, "Cashmere you are what I have always wanted. You have become more than I ever expected. And from the day that I saw you, I wanted to protect you. I wanted to be your bodyguard. I knew that you were special, and I knew that you would make a beautiful wife and mother. I am happy that we kept our love strong and pure, although we were inexperienced and had hiccups. I welcome this privilege to be your husband. I love you with all my heart. I promise to do my best. To help you with your goals. To treasure your honesty. To listen to you. We have been through tough times and so through tough times and good times, I have come to appreciate your spirituality. Your integrity. Your grasp of the foundation of marriage. I want to spend the rest of my life with you."

Cashmere said her vows. "Geronimo, just your name has always aroused excitement, confidence and action. You are the man for me. You and you only are my soul mate. I have always loved you and I have never stopped loving you. Even through tough times, I could not imagine being without you. I have never met another man like you. This time around, I have a better understanding of what marriage is and how to make you love me even more. I am willing to be your complement. To put your interests first. To be a good forgiver. To say I am sorry when I need to.

To say and prove that I love you. I am amazed by your growth and how humble you have become. I cannot fathom spending the rest of my life with anyone other than you. I welcome the privilege to be your wife."

Now that they had said their personal vows, the Justice of the Peace stepped up to complete the vows. This is the main part everyone waited for. This would be very precious for this couple because of what they had gone through and to get to that point of getting married again was miraculous. Many who attended the wedding had been waiting for this day some years. The Justice of the Peace started with Geronimo.

"Geronimo, do you take Cashmere to be your wedded wife, to live together in marriage? Do you promise to love her, comfort her, honor and keep her for better or worse, for richer or poorer, in sickness and health, and forsaking all others, be faithful only to her, for as long as you both shall live?

Geronimo said, "I do." Now it was Cashmere's

turn to answer the questions.

"Cashmere, do you take Geronimo to be your wedded husband, to live together in marriage? Do you promise to love him, comfort him, honor and keep him for better or worse, for richer or poorer, in sickness and health, and forsaking all others, be faithful only to him, for as long as you both shall live?"

Cashmere said, "I do."

After Cashmere said that the Justice of the Peace said, "I now pronounce you husband and wife. Geronimo, you may kiss your bride. What God has yoked together, let no man put apart."

The couple kissed and waved to the zoom guests. The guests clapped their hands and stood up to show their respect to Geronimo and Cashmere after they walked back down the Red Carpet toward the big screen near the patio to get a closer look at their guests. That is where Geronimo grabbed Cashmere and hugged her tighter than he ever remembered doing so before. Then the photographer took their wedding portrait. As they walked closer toward the house, the family of four took more photos. While holding Cashmere's hand in his hand above their heads, Geronimo told his guests that he finally got his baby back. Right after he did that, Cashmere placed Geronimo's hand over her heart, passionately telling the group that she got her soul mate back. Sam called to Malinda, saying that the kind of wedding his parents had was the type of wedding he wanted in this backyard with family and friends. She gave a thumbs up.

Jasmine got everyone's attention before she spoke. She thanked her momma in front of all of the zoom guests for teaching her by word and example how she needed to prepare for marriage. Among all the things that her momma learned from Ms. Hattie was when she read that God hated a divorcing and God wanted marriage mates to cherish His gift, marriage. Then Jasmine concluded that she now understood why

God hated divorce. Her parents loved each other but they just did not know how to be married and if they had prior knowledge of what they learned these past few months from Ms. Hattie, they would have never divorced.

Epilogue

For years after Geronimo and Cashmere remarried, their marriage kept getting stronger and stronger. Cashmere and Geronimo continued with their spiritual counseling sessions with Ms. Hattie and Mr. Daniel. They attributed those counseling sessions to helping them keep a balanced view of material things as well as maintain balance when circumstances change.

Sales from Cashmere's new line of handmade soaps, lotions and deodorants exploded. She could hardly keep up with the orders. A company from Paris, France bought her entire line and hired her to work as a consultant. Geronimo's grandparents signed a power of attorney, so that Geronimo could manage the millions of dollars they made from the oil on their land.

Skyler graduated from college with a degree in English. The very year he graduated from Alabama; the Los Angeles Lakers drafted him. Two years later, The Los Angeles Sparks drafted Jasmine. The couple's first conflict arose when Jasmine decided that she did not want to wear the five-carat engagement ring Skyler had secretly bought for her. Skyler convinced her to wear the ring as a reminder of his love for her. She wore the ring everywhere she went except when she played basketball. They married one year after the Sparks drafted Jasmine. Jasmine retired after nine years of playing professional basketball when she learned they were pregnant with twins. After playing twelve years of professional basketball, Skyler retired. He spent his time with his wife and their twins, Winter and Sage. He authored several poetry books.

Sam and Malinda turned out to be exceptional

artists. Jasmine gave Sam the family's heirloom engagement ring. He and Malinda sold the two-carat engagement ring that Sam had given her. After they married, they used the money to move to Spain where they worked to restore antique paintings.

River and Lillie married shortly after they graduated from college. River received a degree in Journalism. Lillie received a degree in Home Economics. She lost her interest in playing professional basketball because she preferred being a housewife and having a big family. River wrote Jasmine's life story and submitted it to the Monroe Journal. The couple moved to Atlanta where he started working for CNN. Two years after they married, Lillie gave birth to their daughter, Ireland. Two years later, she gave birth to their son, Mason River. Almost one year later she gave birth to their third child, daughter Ellie. Three years later, they had another daughter, Samantha. They enrolled each of their children in dance school at the age of three years old.

Mr. and Mrs. Parish moved to Las Vegas to choreograph dance for some of the dance acts at Caesar's Palace, where they signed a two-year contract. With all of their years of experience, the couple decided to open a dance studio in Atlanta Georgia. That move allowed them to be close to their grandchildren. As mentioned earlier, Lillie and River sent each of their children to dance school when each one was three years old. It worked out fine that River's parents owned the school.

Missy Marshal never disclosed why her family was moving to North Carolina. She maintained that "It was too complicated." She, her husband, Kip, and her son, Shane, stayed in the same house in Monroeville until Shane died of an unknown disease ten years later. After his death, the couple moved to North Carolina.

Coach and Mrs. Van Damme moved to West Palm Beach Florida where he started coaching college basketball. Five years after they married, she ran away to Hollywood.

Tommy was the first person to contract Covid-19 in Monroeville twice. He and Marylou never married. She became the editor for the Mobile Press.

Three years after the older Chadsworth couple remarried, The Atlanta Hawks recruited Coach Chadsworth to work as an assistant basketball coach. Liz remained in Alabama, working as a marriage counselor. She never recovered from jungle fever. When she visited her old job in Bradenton, Florida, she ran into Joe. She learned that Joe was in marriage counseling, and she convinced him to come to her for marriage counseling. She thought that they could pick up where they left off fourteen years ago. Shortly after that, she closed her business in Alabama and moved back to Sarasota-Bradenton where she began working for the NAACP.

Consuelo Danita
loves to write about subjects
that deal with everyday life.
Consuelodanita.com

www.ingramcontent.com/pod-product-compliance
Lightning Source LLC
LaVergne TN
LVHW050914080826
845145LV00001B/78

* 9 7 8 0 9 9 9 4 9 2 6 1 1 *